THE RIVAL BID

DISTINGUISHED GENTLEMEN SERIES

REESE RYAN

Sinfully Sweet Publishing
Fuquay Varina, North Carolina

ReeseRyan.com

Editor: Tam Jernigan
Cover Design: Dot Covers

ACKNOWLEDGMENTS

A special thank you to the ladies of Book Euphoria for conceiving this series and for inviting me to be a part of this amazing anthology. Thank you to my fellow Distinguished Gentleman lit sisters for making this series fun to participate in and phenomenal for the readers. And thank you to all of the incredible readers who have wholly embraced this series.

ABOUT THE RIVAL BID

She'll fight for what she wants...even if she has to make a deal with the devil.

Camilla Anthony painstakingly restores older Chicagoland homes to their former glory. So when the opportunity arises to acquire an abandoned block of homes and a school in her neighborhood of Southlake Park, she's ready to take on the challenge. But she'll need the help of her former crush and frequent real estate rival.

Mekkai Arrington builds luxury homes in urban communities. Increasingly, he and preservationist Camilla Anthony clash over gentrification. But when Kai reluctantly agrees to participate in a charity bachelor auction, Camilla vies for him and wins. She proposes an alliance that will benefit both of their companies while salvaging a historic neighborhood in their childhood community. But will the fiery passion that erupts between them during their beach getaway blow up their deal?

DEAR READER

This was such a fun, but challenging project. I enjoyed every minute spent in the fictional Chicago neighborhood of Southlake Park. It was also nice to take a quick trip to Pleasure Cove—the fictional North Carolina coastal community where my Pleasure Cove series is set.

I fell in love with this story and with Mekkai and Camilla's characters. I hope you'll enjoy your time with them, too.

MEKKAI

"$\mathcal{A}$nd that is what Arrington Builders' can do for the Southlake Park community," Mekkai Arrington said with an air of finality as he closed his impressive Power-Point presentation.

Constance Green, the community development officer of the Southlake Park Revitalization Association, who'd been flirting with him shamelessly throughout the process, jumped to her feet and applauded, prompting the alderman and other community leaders seated at the tables on either side of him to applaud, too. About half of the standing-room-only crowd clapped, though not nearly as enthusiastically. But the other half of the residents gathered in the auditorium of the Southlake Park Cultural Center stared daggers at him and sucked their teeth or rolled their eyes.

Tough crowd.

Clearly, his charm and good looks alone weren't going to be as effective with this crowd as they had been with Ms. Green.

But he hadn't expected this to be easy. Nothing in his life

had been since that awful morning when he was fifteen and had awakened to discover that his world had been shattered.

"Many of you obviously have questions." A warm grin slid across Kai's face as he made eye contact with a few of the scowling women in the crowd.

Two of them relaxed and nodded.

"That's why I'm here." He deepened his smile and spread his palms. "I want to share Arrington Builders' vision for Southlake Park and the surrounding communities with you. But I'm also here to answer your questions and allay any of your concerns."

Ms. Green seemed less than enthusiastic about the prospect of a Q & A. But she invited community residents to line up at the podium to ask their questions about the planned community he hoped to build in Southlake Park.

Forty-five minutes later, he'd answered a variety of questions about the type of homes they'd build. He'd also talked about the projects his company had completed in Chicagoland suburbs over the past year and those completed back in Pleasure Cove, North Carolina, where he'd started his company five years ago.

He'd relaxed when Ms. Green announced that they'd only be entertaining two more questions. But when the final speaker stepped up to the podium, his muscles tensed and he was sure his heart had jumped up into his throat. Suddenly, his head felt as if it was spinning, and the simple act of breathing became a complicated chore.

Cammie.

"I'm Camilla Anthony, owner of Charming Home Design," she said with a sweet smile. But there was something savage in her pretty, chestnut-brown eyes. A look that indicated that she was here to rip his throat open and throw his carcass on the side of the road. "The homes your company has built are beautiful. They're unbelievably luxurious, and the material and craftsmanship are top-notch."

"Thank you, Cam…I mean, Ms. Anthony," he said, with the wariness of a man waiting for the other shoe to drop and crush his skull. "We take great pride in our attention to detail and we don't cut corners."

"Duly noted." Those mesmerizing brown eyes sparkled. She stood taller. Her back arched slightly, revealing a little more of her impressive cleavage.

Little Cammie Anthony is all grown up.

They'd been friends as kids, before his world went to shit, courtesy of her father, Michael Anthony. She was sweet and funny. And she'd had an innocent crush on him. But he was four years older than her, so he'd seen her as more of an honorary little sister.

But his thoughts about the fine-ass woman standing before him now were anything but platonic. They were lustful, bordering on straight-up dirty.

Her rich, cinnamon-brown skin practically glowed. She raked her fingers through her wild mane of shiny, bouncy curls that fell below her shoulders. Camilla sank her teeth into her full, pouty lower lip. And her impressive breasts, framed by her arms resting on the podium, seemed to demand his attention.

"Mr. Arrington?"

Ms. Green stared at him with one eyebrow raised and a hand on her hip. "Ms. Anthony asked you a question."

"Right." Kai loosened his collar and widened his smile. "Please repeat your question, Ms. Anthony."

"How on earth do you expect people in this community to afford your luxury homes?" Her gaze bore into his.

"I realize that not everyone is in the market for a Cadillac, so to speak." He kept his tone light and made eye contact with some of the doubters in the crowd.

He was losing them again. Their arms were folded, and their scowls had returned.

"That's why we'll offer a variety of home layouts to accommodate different budgets and family sizes. And of course, if a family chooses not to go with a top-of-the-line trim package, our basic package will still give them a beautiful, well-made home."

"I've seen the base prices on your homes, Mr. Arrington. Most of them are well above what is affordable for the average Southlake Park resident."

"In addition to the homes we'll be building in this planned community, there will also be a small community of townhomes--"

"Those are priced out of range for many residents, too." She looked at him squarely, her voice passionate, but controlled.

A rising grumble started to spread throughout the room.

"Settle down, please." Ms. Green raised her hands as she looked around the room, then flashed him a worried look. "Let's give Mr. Arrington a chance to respond to your concerns."

Kai stood taller. He narrowed his gaze at Cammie.

He'd rejected her twenty-five years ago, ending their friendship. She'd obviously come here today to get her revenge by sabotaging his first proposed project in Southlake Park. The neighborhood where they'd both grown up.

"Will the homes in this proposed community be out of the price range for some members of the community residents?" Kai asked, then answered. "Yes. But will it add value to the community as a whole, including bringing more retail space, employment opportunities, and taxable income to the community? The answer is also a resounding *yes*."

"The retail space will include stores many residents can't afford to shop in. Those jobs will be minimum-wage retail jobs. And the increased property taxes will negate any other perceived gains," Camilla countered coolly, as the crowd grew more vocal and restless. One corner of her mouth turned up in a barely-perceptible smirk. "What Southlake Park needs isn't more luxury McMansions, Mr. Arrington. It's beautiful, functional, affordable housing that pays homage to this community's rich history. Homes like the ones my company has restored throughout Southlake Park and communities just like it."

She folded her hands on the podium and tilted her head slightly. Her shiny curls spilled to one side. "I realize that it isn't as lucrative a path, Mr. Arrington. But I challenge you to do what's in the best interest of this community, not what's in *your* best interest. Thank you."

When she stepped away from the podium in her casual, but sexy little blue dress, the crowd erupted in thunderous applause. Even from the alderman and community leaders surrounding him.

He released an uneasy sigh and acknowledged Cammie with the jut of his chin as he joined in with an obligatory clap.

Ms. Green brought the meeting to a close, informing the crowd that they weren't prepared to make a decision on the new mixed-use space today. Another town hall meeting would be scheduled to discuss the matter further. In the meantime, the focus should remain focused on current fundraising efforts.

His heart sank. Until Camilla Anthony had stepped up to the podium with her speech, the committee had been putty in his hands. Still, he forced a smile and hung around to answer questions and shake hands. But his gaze returned to Camilla again and again.

He watched from the corner of his eye as she flitted about the room, talking to community residents. Her warm brown skin glowed and her contagious smile practically lit the room. Even from a distance, there was something about her laugh that sent a shock of warmth through his body. He couldn't help thinking back to the afternoons they'd spent together in the offices of the construction company co-owned by their fathers who were once business partners and best friends.

"Well, everything seemed to be going fine until that Anthony woman came along." Ms. Green was suddenly beside him, her gaze cast in Cammie's direction, too. "But it's nothing we can't recover from. Your project will be a fine addition to Southlake Park. The residents will understand once they see those beautiful homes going up."

"I agree." He nodded, not bothering to tear his gaze away from his old friend who'd hugged a woman in the crowd and was now heading for the exit. "Thank you, Green, for your support. Would you excuse me?"

Kai trotted toward the door after Camilla.

He had zero interest in catching up with his old friend or reminiscing over the good old days. The days before everything went to shit and his entire life blew up, while hers went on as golden as ever. No, they needed to talk business.

This wasn't the first time since he'd returned to Chicago that Camilla Anthony had tried to undermine his company's plans.

Hell hath no fury like a woman scorned.

But Kai hadn't pulled up stakes from North Carolina and returned to Chicago just to have Cammie Anthony run interference and undermine his goals. If she had a personal vendetta against him, they were going to hash this out today.

CAMILLA

*C*amilla Anthony rubbed her hands together beneath the hand dryer until the noisy machine shut itself off. She took another glance in the mirror, rearranging a few of the curls that had fallen out-of-place, then reapplied her lip gloss.

Cam stepped out of the bathroom in time to see Kai re-entering the building, his gaze sweeping the hall.

God he's handsome.

Rich, dark brown skin. Dark, piercing eyes. A hint of gray at his temples and in his beard. An incredibly sexy grin that likely had women, like Constance Green, falling at his feet.

He was just over six feet tall. The fabric of his expensive, slim cut gray suit hung perfectly on his lean, muscular frame.

Kai pursed his lips and stroked his beard thoughtfully, and her mind went straight into the gutter, wondering about the taste and feel of those sensual lips.

"Looking for me?" she asked finally stepping out into the hallway.

His eyes widened momentarily, but then he narrowed his gaze and frowned. He loosened his expensive designer tie as he strode toward her. Kai stopped a few feet short of her and shoved his hands in his pockets.

He glanced around them, as if he wasn't thrilled about being seen with the enemy.

"Was that little show you put on in there really necessary?" He leaned closer, his voice low and husky.

Kai's close proximity and the timbre of his voice sent shivers up her spine. His heavenly scent—like clean, fresh cotton with a hint of something masculine she couldn't quite identify—was enticing, but not overpowering. For a brief moment, she wished she could press her nose to his neck and inhale the scent more deeply.

"It was a community meeting. The questions I asked were fair and valid." She shrugged, her eyes never leaving his. "I don't see what the problem is, Mr. Arrington."

"The problem is that..." He heaved a quiet sigh, maintaining his controlled tone with what seemed like great effort. "The problem is that you seem to have made it your mission to interfere in my business, *Ms. Anthony*."

"What happens to Southlake Park is *everyone's* business." She folded her arms and tipped her chin. "Or have you been away so long that you've forgotten that?"

"You're not the only one who wants what's best for the community, Camilla." He heaved an impatient sigh and folded his arms, too. His jaw tensed. "You don't think it kills me to see all the overgrown lots and abandoned homes in Southlake Park?"

She shrugged. "I don't know. This isn't really your neighborhood any more, is it?"

It was a low blow. Even she realized that, but she couldn't resist taking a jab at him.

From the tension in his jaw and the narrowing of his gaze, she'd hit her target.

"Southlake Park will *always* be my home," Kai seethed, his stare intense.

"Well it *is* my home, and it always has been."

"Save the selfless saint act for your adoring fans in there. You've got them convinced that you're doing this strictly for Southlake Park. Bravo." He clapped twice sarcastically. "But you and I both know that your goal is to run a competing home builder out of the neighborhood."

"I'm not a home builder. I'm a preservationist," she clarified. "I restore the homes in our community to their former glory, not tear them down to make way for cookie-cutter McMansions."

His jaw tensed in response to the dig and anger flashed behind his dark eyes. "Okay, Cam, let's discuss what this is *really* about. Revenge."

"Don't flatter yourself, Arrington." She shifted her gaze from his momentarily. "I was an affordable housing community activist long before you returned to Chicago."

"Maybe." He acknowledged with a nod, then stepped closer. "But this feels deliberate. Personal. Like payback for ending our friendship."

"That was twenty-five years ago, Kai. I was eleven-years-old. Do you really think I'm that petty?" Even as she said it, the pain of that day burned in her chest. No one had ever hurt her more. Before or since. "Besides, you're overestimating the value of our friendship. It certainly didn't mean much to you."

Kai grimaced, shifting his gaze from hers momentarily.

"Look, Cam, I know that the way things went down between us was pretty fucked up. But I was fifteen and angry as hell. My entire life fell apart and it was all..." He let his words trail off. "I know it wasn't your fault personally, but--"

"But you still blame my father for the mistakes *your father* made?" Cam winced, tears sting her eyes. "I can't believe you honestly still blame my dad for what happened."

Kai folded his arms and the stony expression returned to his face. He didn't respond. He didn't need to.

"I'm sorry about everything that happened to your family, too." She forced her gaze to meet his, determined not to shed the tears that burned her eyes. "What happened was...awful. And none of it was your fault either. But regardless of our past and the history between our dads...that isn't why I'm doing this. If you were any other builder, making the proposal you're making now, my reaction would be exactly the same."

His dubious expression indicated he wasn't buying it. Thankfully, he was interrupted before he could question her further.

"Mr. Arrington, there you are." Constance Green approached, giving Cam a side-eye. "I'm glad I caught you before you left. A few of the local shopkeepers have questions about your plans for the new retail space."

"I'd be happy to address their concerns." Kai gave the woman a broad smile. He turned back to Cam, the smile gone. "Good night, Ms. Anthony. I've no doubt our paths will cross again."

As soon as he was out of earshot, Camilla released a long, heavy sigh, her hands shaking.

As long as Mekkai Arrington was hell-bent on gentrifying this community, they most certainly would.

Old wounds and overwhelming attraction aside, she wouldn't stop fighting to protect Southlake Park.

MEKKAI

*K*ai pulled up to the home that his company was building in Ravenswood, the same Chicago neighborhood where he currently resided. The same neighborhood where his father had moved his family when the construction company he'd co-owned with Cammie's father had been booming.

He got out of his jet-black metallic Porsche Cayenne and studied the sprawling two-story brick home. They were in the final phase of the renovation project. He greeted the husband and wife team of landscapers who'd already begun planting flowers and shrubbery. Then he made his way into the first floor of the beautifully-renovated home.

"How's it going, Ahmad?" Kai stood beside his crew chief, Ahmad Kaleel.

"Morning, boss." The man tipped his chin without taking his eyes off the two-man crew installing the stainless-steel appliances, including a chef-grade stove. Ahmad's thick arms were folded tightly over his barrel chest and his rigid stare dared the men to damage the freshly-painted walls and expensive white cabinets or chip the newly installed black granite waterfall. "Rick and Sandy are putting in the land-scape. The appliances finally arrived. Ned is nearly finished with the fireplace, and the fellas are out back, laying the tile on the patio."

"The staircase came out beautifully." Kai ran his hand along the metal banister of the floating staircase with its wooden treads.

"It did." Ahmad finally shifted his gaze from the appliance installation crew. "And they finished ahead of schedule, which means we're back on track and should have this place ready for the open house in a little over a week."

"Great, I'm going to take a look at that ceiling in the master bedroom, before I head over to the duplex in Ander-sonville." Kai headed for the stairs.

"How'd the community meeting go last night?" Ahmad asked.

"Honestly?" Kai froze, then turned slowly to meet the man's gaze. He dragged a hand through his hair and shrugged. "It could go either way. But I'm not waiting around to see what happens. I'm looking for my next project."

"Good. Because I just heard something that might be of interest." Ahmad looked around, then indicated that they should continue the discussion upstairs, away from the crew. They went up to the master bedroom suite with its newly completed tiled ceiling and Ahmad closed the door. "I heard about a possible deal you might be interested in. A block of six homes on a cul-de-sac and an abandoned school."

"Where?" Kai asked, regarding the man with interest.

A rare smile spread across Ahmad's face. "Southlake Park."

"Really?" Kai stroked his beard. "Who's selling the proper-ties? The bank?"

"No." The man's smile widened even more. "It's a project that Lamberton Construction took on."

Uncle Lou.

Though he ran a competing construction company, Louis Lamberton had been good friends with both Kai's father and Cammie's. So close that both of them called him Uncle Lou. He still considered Lou family. But with his busy schedule, he'd only managed to visit with the older man a handful of times since he'd returned to Chicago a year ago.

"And they're looking to sell? Why?"

Ahmad shrugged. "Seems like he's in over his head."

The residents of Southlake Park were reluctant to jump on board with his proposal to create a large, planned community of high-end homes. But this smaller project was the perfect way to give them a taste of what they'd be getting. The homes would be a showcase in the community that would attract residents with higher incomes and provide additional property taxes.

"That could be a really good look for us."

Ahmad nodded. "If you're interested, I'd strike quick. I heard this from my cousin, who works on one of his crews. But old man Lamberton hasn't made it public, yet. So if you approach him now--"

"I can avoid a bidding war." Kai tapped the man's shoulder with the back of his hand. "Good looking out, Ahmad. Get me an address. I'll swing by and look at the properties, then try to get a meeting with Lou Lamberton later today."

"If he's under financial pressure to sell the properties, maybe you can get the whole package for a steal."

"I won't lowball him," Kai said firmly. "I want the property at a good deal, but a fair one."

"Of course." Ahmad fished a scrap of paper out of his pocket and handed it to Kai. "The deal would include all six houses on Marigold Circle and the nearby abandoned school. All of the addresses are there."

Kai clamped a hand on the man's shoulder and grinned. "Thank you for this." He held up the wrinkled piece of paper.

"And for the job you've done here. You're an outstanding crew chief. Everything looks great."

Ahmad thanked him and returned to his job while Kai inspected the remaining upstairs bedrooms and an office. His phone rang and he pulled it out of his pocket.

Mama Peaches.

Kai smiled. Mama Peaches was the grand dame of South-lake Park. Had been for as long as he could remember. The older woman knew everyone in the community and had an opinion about everything, which she was never shy about sharing. But more importantly, Mama Peaches had been a second mother to him. She'd taken care of him and his younger brother Keith when their own mother had been unable to. He and Keith were just two of the dozens of young men Mama Peaches had cared for over the years.

"Mama Peaches. How are you?"

"Hmm..." She huffed. "A woman could shrivel up and die waiting on you to return her call."

"C'mon, Mama Peaches." He laughed. "I know I've been busy, but I'm not that bad. Besides, we just saw each other at the meeting last night."

"A rushed hello and a peck on the cheek does not count as a conversation, gent," she said sternly, invoking the nickname she called the young men she helped raise. It was her way of reminding them of the importance of behaving as a gentle-man. Respectful, honest, and chivalrous. "And the last time we had an actual conversation was at least two weeks ago," she said emphatically. "And I'm the one who called you."

"Yes, ma'am," Kai said contritely.

Mama Peaches was an important part of his life. If it hadn't been for her, he and Keith would've been shipped off to live with relatives out of state, separating them from their mother who'd been hospitalized. If Mama Peaches hadn't stepped in and taken them in, he and Keith would likely have been sent to different foster homes. God knows what might've happened to them.

"I'm sorry I've been so preoccupied. What can I do for you, Mama Peaches?"

"You know *exactly* what you can do for me," she said. "Isn't that why you've been avoiding my calls?"

Kai chuckled. Mama Peaches wasn't wrong.

"This bachelor auction is an essential piece of the South-lake Park restoration fundraising efforts," she reminded him. "When I asked you, you promised to think about it. You been thinking long enough?" she asked.

Kai drew in a deep breath and sighed. Mama Peaches. How could he possibly turn her down?

"All right, Mama P." He forced a smile, in spite of his aver-sion to the idea of strutting across a stage and being bid on like cattle. "For you, I'll do it."

"Thank you, baby. I knew you wouldn't let me down." She chuckled. "But you aren't just doing this for me. You're doing it for all of Southlake Park. And from the temperature in that room last night, seems like a little goodwill might go a long way toward getting folks onboard with that building project of yours."

Mama Peaches was right, as always.

If Camilla Anthony doubted his commitment to South-lake Park, surely other residents did, too. Especially the old guard.

Folks old enough to remember when the scandal with his father had erupted twenty-five years ago. People who'd closely followed the trial and watched his father being carted off to prison. People who either turned up their noses at the name Arrington or still regarded him and his brother with pity. Both of which made him feel like that fifteen-year-old boy reliving the entire nightmare all over again.

Before they said goodbye, Mama Peaches promised to get

him all of the info he would need to participate in the South-lake Park Bachelor Auction.

Kai reminded himself of exactly why he'd returned to Chicago. He'd come back determined to restore his family's name and his father's legacy. And he wouldn't let anyone get in the way of that, not even Camilla Anthony.

He said goodbye to his work crew and returned to his truck to drive the short distance to another renovation project in Andersonville. Alone with his thoughts, he couldn't get the image of Cammie out of his head.

She was beautiful and brilliant. A self-assured firecracker who wasn't easily dissuaded. Qualities he'd admired when they were childhood friends. Wrap those traits up in the incredibly sexy package she'd become, and his pulse had raced the moment he laid eyes on her.

But despite the carnal thoughts he'd had about fine-ass Cammie Anthony, there was just too much bad history between their families. As kids, they'd been caught up in the war between their fathers, standing on opposite sides of a chasm, with no room for compromise in between.

Time had done little to heal the deep wounds they'd both sustained. Cruelly, history was repeating itself. Only now, instead of fighting over whose father was the liar and thief, they were battling for the soul of Southlake Park.

The last round had gone to the Anthonys, but this time the Arringtons would come out on top.

CAMILLA

"Uncle Lou!" Camilla hugged her father's oldest friend, Louis Lamberton. A man she loved more than the uncles with whom she shared DNA. "It's good to see you."

"You, too, sugar." He regarded her with a warm smile. Nearly seventy, the man was still incredibly handsome. "What brings you by the office? Aren't you and your crew working on a restoration project today?"

"We're just about finished with the reno over in Logan Square. I'm looking for my next project, so I thought I'd see if there were any deals you've passed on that might be right for me."

The man grimaced, his gaze shifting toward the floor as his wiry gray brows gathered.

"What's wrong, Uncle Lou?" Camilla squeezed his hand.

"You hungry?" he asked, ignoring her question. "Dora sent enough chicken salad to feed an army."

"I'd love some." She took her coat off and hung it on one of the hooks by the door. "But let me make it."

Camilla indulged Uncle Lou's small talk as she prepared

them both chicken salad sandwiches and grabbed two cans of blackberry-flavored carbonated water. It was the only way Aunt Dora had been able to get him to stop drinking soda after his diabetes diagnosis several years ago.

He joined her at the battered, wobbly round table in the break area.

"So..." she asked after they'd both eaten a few bites in silence. "What was that look about? Seriously, Uncle Lou, is everything okay with you and Aunt Dora? She seemed sad when I spoke with her earlier today."

That seemed to break his heart even more and she nearly regretted asking. But Uncle Lou and Aunt Dora were family. Proud, stubborn, and independent. But family, nonetheless. So she had no intention of leaving until he'd leveled with her.

"That cul-de-sac and school I bought up on Magnolia Circle..." He sighed and lowered his gaze again, then shrugged. "I need to unload it. It's just too big a project for me to take on right now."

"Are you okay?" Camilla's heartbeat thudded in her ears. The pained expression on the man's face answered the question before he opened his mouth to say a single word.

"I've been having some chest pains for several weeks. Dora finally made me go to the doctor. Turns out, I've been having mild heart attacks."

"Oh my God." She clamped a hand over her mouth, her eyes immediately stinging with tears. "What are you doing at work? Shouldn't you be at the hospital or at home resting?"

"I promised Dora that I'd take it easy. That's why I'm here at the office. She was worried I'd get too worked up on a job. I'm taking my medication, just as the doctor prescribed." Lou patted his breast pocket and pills jiggled in a bottle. "And I'm bringing someone on to handle the day-to-day operations for a bit. But in the meantime--"

"That project is just too big for you to take on now."

Camilla nodded in agreement. "Aunt Dora's right, Uncle Lou. I'm glad you're listening to her."

She wiped her hands on a napkin. "And maybe I can take one or two of those houses off your hands. I'd need to see them first, of course."

"I appreciate the offer, baby girl." He placed his large, warm hand on hers, using the nickname her father sometimes still called her. "But I think I can get more for the properties if I keep them together in a single block."

Cammie couldn't disagree. Buying the entire block plus the school would be an excellent opportunity for the right company. Only...

"What is it, Cam?" He tilted his head as he studied her frown.

"I'm worried. About you and about what's going to happen to all those properties. With you, I trusted that they'd be restored and remain affordable. But if you sell them to the highest bidder--"

"I know." He nodded solemnly. "It's something I considered, too. That's why I'm willing to take less if a company will commit to making the housing block affordable to members of our community."

"Do you really think anyone would go for a stipulation like that?" She nibbled on her fingernail despite having a perfectly good half-eaten chicken salad sandwich in front of her.

He shrugged and took another bite of his sandwich. "I don't know. But I'm willing to sit on the property for a month or two to try to find a deal that's right for the community."

"Can I see the specs on the deal and what you hope to get for it?"

"Sure." He left the cafeteria, returning with a manila envelope. He slid it across the table then took a swig of his sparkling water. "Why? What are you thinking? Do you have a company in mind?"

Cam didn't answer him. She just studied the photos and the descriptions of each home and the proposed renovations. When she got to the final page, she checked the figure circled in black pen.

It took her breath away.

The number was substantial. But in light of how many properties were included in the package and what each renovated unit would command, the deal would be highly-profitable. Even if the homes were sold at an affordable price.

She'd built a good, reliable team that did incredible work. They were quickly making a name for themselves all over the Chicagoland area. But in order to take on a project of this magnitude, she'd have to expand considerably. Then there was the matter of financing. Would the small bank she dealt with be willing to loan her this much?

"I can see the wheels turning in that beautiful brain of yours." Lou took another bite of his sandwich. "Don't keep me in suspense. Tell me what you're thinking."

Camilla blew out a slow breath and closed the folder. She laced her fingers together on top of it. "I'm thinking you should sell to me."

"C'mon, Cam. I already told you that I don't want to break the block up, if I don't have to."

"I'm not asking you to break up the package, Uncle Lou. I'm asking you to sell me the entire thing." She studied his response.

His brows furrowed, forming deep creases that spanned across his forehead. He raked his thick fingers through his thinning white and gray hair. "Camilla, I appreciate what you're trying to do here. I know you want to help me out, but this is a big undertaking."

"My team can handle it." Her voice was shaky. She pressed

her hands firmly to the table and sat taller, erasing the uncertainty that was in her voice moments before. "You've seen what we can do."

"You do amazing work, Camilla. No one can deny that. But this project...it's a whole 'nother animal. You've never taken on a project this big." His eyes and tone were apologetic.

"True, but there's a first time for everything, right? I'll never know what I can accomplish if I don't take the chance."

"What about the financing? You don't have this kind of money on hand, and I'm familiar with your bank. They'll be reluctant to give you a loan this big."

That eliminated any chance that he'd consider offering seller financing on the block of properties. But then again, she couldn't blame him. After financing several of his youngest son Landis's business ventures, Lou had sworn he'd never do business with a family member or close friend again.

"Okay, well then I'll just have to get an investor."

Lou folded his arms and narrowed his gaze, one furry brow nearly meeting what was left of his hairline.

"Fine, I'll get several investors to go in on the property," she conceded.

"Investors want *maximum* profits, Camilla. They won't want to do a first-time deal with you where you're knee-capping their profits." He rubbed his forehead. "I have no doubt you'll be routinely doing deals of this magnitude one day. But that day, Cam, is not today. I'm sorry, sweetheart."

He patted her arm solemnly.

"I guess not." She forced a sad smile and nibbled on her sandwich.

Lou's phone rang and he excused himself to take the call.

Camilla slumped against the back of her chair and slowly finished her sandwich.

She adored her Uncle Lou, but she couldn't help wondering if he wouldn't have been more amenable to the idea if he didn't still see her as Mike Anthony's *baby girl*.

But she was nothing, if not determined. And as long as Lou Lamberton's property was for sale, she would focus on putting together a deal so that she'd be the one to buy it.

MEKKAI

"*T*hank you for meeting me on such short notice, Uncle Lou." Kai shook the older man's hand.

"You called from the parking lot." The older man chuckled, then gestured toward the chair in front of his desk before taking a seat behind it. "Besides, the matter sounded pretty urgent."

Kai sat, his knee bouncing slightly. He cared deeply for the old man and he in no way wanted to embarrass him.

Lou Lamberton and his wife hadn't taken him and Keith in when their mother had taken ill, but he'd made sure that they didn't want for anything.

By the time his mother had recovered, the bank had already repossessed their expensive home in Ravenswood. His mother couldn't bear living in the city where their family had suffered so much pain and humiliation. She wanted to give them a fresh start. So she moved them down to Pleasure Cove, North Carolina. The small, coastal beach town where she'd been born.

Uncle Lou had continued to send them what he could until Kai's mother had gotten on her feet.

"Whatever you've come to say has you all twisted up in knots. What is it, Mekkai?" Lou steepled his hands on the desk in front of him, the lines of his face creased with worry. "Is your mother all right?"

"Ma's doing great."

"And your brother?" Lou inquired.

"Keith is fine, too." Kai wiped his damp palms down the legs of his gray cargo pants. "This isn't about me or anyone really. I just..." He cleared his throat and straightened in his seat. "I had a chance to ride by the properties you bought over on that cul-de-sac on Marigold Circle. I noticed that you haven't started the project yet. Have you changed your mind about it?"

Lou sat back in his chair and regarded him warily. He placed his steepled fingers over his belly. "Why do you ask?"

"I'd like to buy the block. All of it."

"What makes you think I want to sell?"

"Does it matter?" He wouldn't lie to Uncle Lou, but he wouldn't throw Ahmad and his cousin under the bus either.

Lou sighed heavily, his eyes squeezing shut momentarily. He folded his arms and shook his head. "Sorry, son. As much as I'd like to, I can't sell the property to you."

"But you *are* selling it?" Kai clarified.

Lou nodded somberly.

"Then why not sell it to me?"

"I bought those properties because I wanted to do something special for this community. Something Southlake Park can be proud of." Lou tapped a finger on his desk for emphasis. "If I sold to you--"

"Are you saying the homes I build wouldn't add value to the neighborhood?"

"No, son. Of course not. You build incredible luxury homes. And the craftsmanship I've seen in some of them...well, it's about the best I've seen anywhere."

"So you're worried that I can't afford it?"

"No, I have no doubt that you can pull together a generous cash deal on the project. But be honest. What would your game plan for the project be?"

Kai had an unsettling feeling in his stomach. Still, he wouldn't lie to Uncle Lou.

He shrugged. "I'd need to go inside the properties to say for sure, but the school I'd definitely tear down. Probably a couple of the houses, too. It'd be cheaper to start from scratch."

Lou nodded, a pained look on his face. "That's what I thought."

"What difference does it make once you've sold it? Did you buy the property with a stipulation not to demolish any of it?" Kai perched his elbow on the armrest of the chair and stroked his beard.

"I made a promise to the community when I bought those properties that I would preserve this block of homes and the old school. That I would turn it into a shining example of what this neighborhood once was and what it could be again." Lou dragged a hand over his head. "And I'm gonna do my damnedest to keep that promise."

"Uncle Lou, new construction isn't the devil. Neither is diversifying the neighborhood by creating high-end homes that appeal to a more affluent clientele."

"Diversifying the neighborhood. Hmm. You mean *gentrifying* the neighborhood. Pushing all the old folks out because they can't afford these prices."

For the first time in Kai's memory, the old man looked at him as if he were bitterly disappointed. Something he hadn't even done when Kai had acted out during those months after the death of his father.

"Don't you see how they're hurting the old neighborhood? Turning it into something folks can't even afford no more?"

He sounded just like Cammie had last night. Had Uncle Lou been at the meeting and he'd simply overlooked him?

"Remember the Jacksons, the Hunters, and the Dixons who lived on your block before you all moved to Ravenswood?"

"Sure. What about them?"

"Every single one of those families were driven out of Southlake Park because they couldn't afford the neighborhood anymore. Some of them couldn't afford the suburbs either."

"Where are they now?" Kai asked tentatively. Almost afraid to hear the answer.

"The Jacksons had to move to a real bad part of town. Lost their oldest boy in a drive-by. The Hunters lived in their car for a year before they finally moved out-of-state. And the Dixons moved in with relatives until they can save up to buy another home."

Kai's chin dipped to his chest, his posture slumped, and he averted the man's gaze.

He shouldn't feel guilty. He wasn't doing anything wrong. Yet, for the first time, he questioned the impact his plans would have on the neighborhood and its residents.

"Maybe we can come to some kind of compro--"

"Did you forget about me in there?" Cammie floated into the room smelling of jasmine. Her dark curls were pulled back into a low ponytail. A slouchy graphic T-shirt that read *I am my ancestors greatest dreams* fell off one shoulder, exposing her dewy, cinnamon brown skin. And the black athletic leggings she wore showed off every curve of her round, plump ass.

Kai swallowed hard, his throat dry. He opened his mouth to speak, but nothing came out.

When she noticed him, she didn't offer so much as a head

nod. Camilla turned her back to him and faced Lou. "Sorry, I didn't realize you had a guest. I'll grab my jacket and go."

"No, Camilla, you don't need to go." Lou held up a hand. Then suddenly he went still and, his head tilted. He looked at Cammie, then at Kai, then back at Cammie again. He turned to Kai. "Maybe we can come up with a compromise."

"You're kidding?" Kai's eyes widened. "Seriously?"

"A compromise on what?" Cammie asked simultaneously, her hand propped on her hip, drawing his attention to the luscious curves she'd acquired in the years since they'd been estranged.

He shook his head and dragged a hand down his face.

Not gonna happen. Ever.

"I'm seriously interested, Uncle Lou. Think about it and give me a call." And please send Aunt Dora my love." Kai exited Lou's office and headed back to his Porsche Cayenne.

He may be a lot of things. But crazy enough to get mixed up in a deal with Camilla Anthony was *not* one of them.

CAMILLA

"*W*hat was *that* about?" Camilla sank onto the chair that Kai had vacated. The seat was still warm and a hint of his cologne lingered. A shudder crawled up her spine.

Damn Kai looked good.

No, he looked more than good. He was gorgeous. As sexy as he'd looked in that suit last night at the town hall meeting, he'd somehow managed to look even more delicious in a casual shirt that clung to his muscular frame and a pair of work pants.

"He wants to buy that block of properties I need to sell off," he announced, assessing her reaction.

"You'd sell it to him, but not to me?" Cammie sat up ramrod straight in the chair, her feet pressed to the floor. "If you sell it to him, you know what he's going to do."

"Calm down, Camilla." He raised a hand and gave her a wary look that reminded her to respect her elders. "Didn't say I would sell to him. Only that he wants me to."

"Then what was that talk about compromising?" Cammie gripped the armrest of the chair, her knees bouncing.

"First, I want you to hear me out *without interruption*." He leaned forward, perching his elbows on the desk.

"I'm listening."

He drew in a deep breath, then quietly sighed. "I know what you can do with this project. That you'd create something beautiful, but affordable. Something that would make this community truly proud." His eyes gleamed and the corners of his mouth lifted in a sad smile. "But it's more than your crew can handle alone. And quite frankly, we both know that while you're a creative genius, the business side of things isn't your strong suit."

Her cheeks stung, and she lowered her gaze. She'd promised not to interrupt. But the truth was that even if she could, she had no real defense. He was right. Uncle Lou had helped her out of a jam more than once because she hadn't had her shit together where her business was concerned.

She had an assistant now who was helping her get everything in order. Someone she'd finally hired at Uncle Lou's urging.

Camilla returned her gaze to the older man's. He seemed satisfied that she hadn't objected to what they both knew to be the truth.

"Kai's company is big enough to handle the project and they do outstanding work. I've no doubt that the homes he'd build would be beautiful and well-made. But they'd be priced out of the range of most of the folks 'round here. We already have enough of that going on."

She nodded enthusiastically, saying a silent *Amen*.

"I promised to make this new community both beautiful and affordable," he continued. "Seems like the only way I can ensure that happens is for the two of you to work together on this project."

Camilla's jaw dropped and her eyes widened. Her pulse

raced at the mere thought of collaborating with Kai Arrington professionally.

"Well? What do you think?" Uncle Lou sat back in his chair and steepled his hands over his belly.

"You can't be serious, Uncle Lou. Arrington Builders is the antithesis of everything I'm trying to do with Anthony RestorationCharming Home Design. Not to mention that Kai's an ass."

"I noticed that you didn't greet him when you came into the room." He frowned. "I know he hurt your feelings when everything was going on with his dad. He was young, and he was deeply hurt and angry. In some ways, he still is. But your families were once good friends. Dora and I'd hoped that you two would've come around by now."

"I didn't shoot the first round." She leaned back and folded her arms. "He did."

"I understand that." He nodded. "But you're one of the kindest, most compassionate people I know. I'd hoped that you could manage to spare at least a little of that for an old friend who obviously needs it." Uncle Lou didn't sound angry. Instead, he sounded profoundly disappointed, which was so much worse.

Her cheeks heated and she avoided his pleading stare. "Look, I think it's wonderful that you've maintained a relationship with both my family and his, despite all of the mess that went down between our fathers. I've always admired your kindness and compassion. But what you're asking of me..."

"I realize that it's a monumental request. That you'd be making a great sacrifice. But I'm not asking you to do this for me. I'm asking you to consider it for Southlake Park--the community we both love."

"How would this even work? And how could I possibly trust him?"

"I can help you two negotiate the deal. And Kai isn't his father, Camilla. The man's word is his bond. And when it comes to his business, he doesn't play. If he agrees to our terms, we can trust him to abide by them. I'm confident of that."

Well, that makes one of us.

"Even if I was willing to give it a try, and I'm not saying that I am, it certainly didn't seem like Kai was onboard."

It was juvenile of her not to acknowledge Kai when she walked into the room. She realized that. Still, her pride was hurt that he patently rejected the idea of working with her and couldn't get away from her fast enough.

It'd been easy to maintain the animosity between them when she hadn't seen him in more than two decades and only thought of him in passing. But seeing him last night transformed her into that silly preteen who'd had a crazy crush on the incredibly handsome and undeniably cool Mekkai Arrington. Her body tingled at the memory of their encounter.

That, too, was problematic.

"Which means that if you're on board with the idea, we're going to have to convince Kai that this is a win for everyone."

"Sorry, Uncle Lou." She stood and put on her jacket. "I gave up trying to convince Kai that I'm on his side a long time ago." She leaned down and kissed the man's cheek. "Thanks for lunch. Promise me you'll take care of yourself."

"I will." He nodded sadly, squeezing her hand. "But promise me that you'll give the idea honest consideration. This is business. Try to leave emotion out of it. You'll see that this is a great opportunity for everyone."

"Fine. It'll give me more time to create a list of all the reasons that Kai and me working together is a terrible idea." Her mouth quirked in a half smile.

Camilla returned to her car but didn't start the ignition

right away. She hated that seeing Kai Arrington still had an effect on her. She hated that she found his flawless brown skin and dark curls enticing. That she couldn't stop imagining what it would feel like to caress his skin or run her fingers through his hair.

She was angry at herself for being fascinated by how damn good he looked in a full beard laced with streaks of gray. That she hadn't been able to tear her focus from his luscious, full lower lip. That she dreamed of gently sinking her teeth into it and kissing him.

The boy who'd been her friend had turned into an unreasonable asshole who couldn't see past his father's lies. Even after the man had been convicted of theft, embezzlement and laundering money for an organized crime family.

The man she'd encountered twice in the past two days, was still in denial where his father was concerned.

So why should she be the one who had to forgo her pride and try to bury the ax between their families? She hadn't done anything wrong. She'd only tried to be his friend despite the shitstorm his father had created. One that nearly swallowed her family whole, too.

But she was ready to take Anthony Preservation-Charming Home Design to the next level. And a project like this would go a long way to helping her achieve that.

Cammie turned the ignition and put the car in gear, heading toward one of the addresses she'd seen in that folder. She had no intention of saying yes to Uncle Lou's proposal. But it couldn't hurt to look.

CAMILLA

*I*t'd been a few days since Uncle Lou proposed that Cammie collaborate with Kai on the Marigold Circle cul-de-sac project. She'd visited the properties that day and been intrigued by the possibilities. Then she'd discussed the prospect with her team. They'd been thrilled. Now she was onboard with the idea, but Kai was still patently against it.

She wouldn't beg Kai to work with her, but she was prepared to convince him that this project could be a victory for both of their companies and the community of Southlake Park.

Kai didn't give a damn about helping her, but he was obviously determined to make a name for himself and his company in Chicago. She could help him with that. But thus far, he hadn't returned her calls.

Her cell phone rang. *Uncle Lou.*

"Any luck getting a sit-down with Kai?" he asked in lieu of a greeting.

"Nada. I left him two messages in the last two days. He hasn't returned either."

"I see." The disappointment in his voice was evident. "Well, I happen to know he's heading over to Hammond Deli for lunch and he's alone. Might be a good place to--"

"Ambush him?"

"I was gonna say catch up with him." Lou chuckled. "Sounds a lot less combative. And, Cam, if you're serious about trying to bring Kai onboard--"

"I need to take it down a notch." *Or three.* "It'll be fine. I've got this, Uncle Lou. Thanks for the tip."

"Good luck, Camilla."

She got in the left lane and headed back toward Hammond Drive, the heart of Southlake Park. Her pulse raced and her heart beat a little faster.

The last time she and Kai had faced off, she been ready to do battle with her nemesis. She'd relished making him squirm, spurred by the pain and humiliation she'd felt the day he'd told her they were no longer friends and that he never wanted to see her again.

The day he'd broken her heart and crushed her soul.

It was twenty-five years ago, and the memory of that day still hurt. But if she had any chance of convincing Kai to go along with her plan, she'd have to revisit their painful past and draw on the memories of their friendship. Make it clear that she would put aside their differences, if he would.

But as she drew closer to the restaurant, the knot in her stomach tightened with dread. She was both titillated and terrified by the prospect of seeing Kai Arrington again.

MEKKAI

Kai entered Hammond Deli and joined the long queue of hungry patrons. The walls, plastered with old photos of celebrities who'd visited the place over the years, testified to the fact that Hammond Deli had been a staple of Southlake Park since long before he'd been born.

The smell of corned beef on rye, hot pastrami, and freshly-made Irish potato soup filled the space. His stomach growled in protest of his decision to take a late lunch.

On the community bulletin board, there was a flyer for the bachelor auction Mama Peaches had roped him into.

So much for hoping this event will be low-key.

He sent a text message to check in with his assistant, Marla, back at the office.

Everything good?

After a few minutes, she sent a reply.

Camilla Anthony called you again. Didn't leave a message this time.

Good. Perhaps Camilla had finally gotten the point.

He had no desire to work with her. Partnering with Michael Anthony was the mistake that had done his father in, leading to his arrest and eventual death in prison. Jailed for a crime he didn't commit.

Camilla Anthony had shown up at that town hall meeting and all but single-handedly derailed his proposal for a planned community in Southlake Park. Now she and Lou expected him to suddenly forget that she'd sabotaged his plans and form an alliance with her?

Uncle Lou and Cammie must be losing it. But then, apparently, so was he.

Camilla Anthony was the last woman on earth he should be attracted to. And yet, she was all he'd been able to think about since the night he'd laid eyes on her at the town hall meeting.

He couldn't stop seeing her gorgeous face. The wild mane of curls that had been an instant turn-on. Or the banging body on display in that fitted dress. Then there were the skin-tight, athletic leggings that clung to every inch of her tantalizing curves when he'd seen her at Uncle Lou's. Seeing her in those damn leggings had made his heart stop and his temperature rise. He hadn't been able to get away from her fast enough.

Thoughts of her had filled his head at the most inconvenient times. Even now, he could hear her voice and smell the faint scent of jasmine that emanated from her dewy skin.

"Still a fan of pastrami and Swiss on rye?"

Kai was almost relieved to discover that Cammie was actually standing beside him in the deli. That he hadn't conjured up her scent and the sound of her voice. He neither smiled nor frowned. Instead, he returned his attention to the chalkboard listing today's specials.

"I've upgraded to Havarti cheese. Got a problem with that, too?" He gave her a side eye, his jaw clenched. "Maybe you'd like to take the podium and explain to everyone here why my consumption of Havarti is problematic enough to send the whole damn neighborhood into a tailspin."

She folded her arms and her body tensed. Her eyes drifted closed momentarily. He was sure she was silently counting to ten.

"Maybe I deserved that," she conceded calmly, her voice quiet. "I know you think the point of my speech at the town hall meeting was to hurt you. But I have no desire to sabotage your business. I'm thrilled that you're doing so well. My only objective is to protect this neighborhood."

Kai turned to stare down at her, his arms folded. "Why are you here, Camilla?"

She took a deep breath and seemed to absorb the blow of his words. The implication that he wished she was anywhere but here. "You know why I'm here, Kai. We need to have a serious conversation about Lou's proposal that we collaborate."

"Thought I'd made my feelings on that pretty clear."

"I had the same reaction initially, believe me. But Uncle Lou made some great points. This could be beneficial for both of us and the community."

"Sir, can I take your order?" The young woman behind the counter asked.

"Let me buy you lunch, and we can talk." She placed a warm hand on his forearm. "Please?"

Cammie was as persistent now as she'd been as that young girl who'd insisted on tagging along with him and his brother. The girl wouldn't take no for an answer when their fathers hadn't wanted to teach her how to paint or lay tile like the boys.

Kai stroked his beard and sighed wearily. "Once we hit that booth, you've got exactly thirty minutes."

"Deal."

Her eyes twinkled and one corner of her mouth turned up in a mischievous smile that momentarily disarmed him. Loosened the rusted lock that kept his heart safe by not letting anyone else in.

Don't fall for it, Kai. And definitely don't fall for her.

CAMILLA

*T*hey'd settled into the booth and each taken a bite of their food.

"Mmm..." Camilla moaned after her first bite. The flavors of the hot pastrami, melted Havarti, stadium mustard, and artisanal rye bread melded for an explosion of taste on her tongue.

When she glanced across the table, Kai was staring at her, his gaze heated.

He quickly shifted his attention to his plate. "You plan to blow the entire thirty minutes oohing and aahing over your food? You've got twenty-five minutes now."

Camilla inhaled a deep breath. *Ten. Nine. Eight. Seven. Six. Five. Four...* Then she reluctantly returned her sandwich to its plate, licking bits of pastrami and melted Havarti from her fingers.

Kai's intense stare took her by surprise. A flush of heat swept down her spine and settled in the space between her thighs. For a moment every thought left her head except one.

God he's handsome. What would it feel like to kiss him?

Okay, maybe that was two thoughts. And had she said

that aloud? He hadn't reacted, other than to steal a glance at his watch and then take another bite of pastrami.

The man even chewed sexy.

And that beard... She'd never been fond of beards. But there was something so perfect about Kai's, connected to a slim, well-groomed mustache. It was full, but not James Harden, lost-in-the-woods-with-no-grooming-tools full. She didn't look at it and wonder if there were bits of food or small woodland creatures lost in it.

"You know you're staring, right." Kai's mouth curved in a cocky, one-sided grin. He sipped his cranberry juice. "I thought you wanted to talk about Uncle Lou's proposal."

That snapped everything back into focus for her.

She tucked a few strands of her curly, chestnut brown hair behind one ear. "I understand the reasons you don't want to work with me on this, Kai. Quite honestly, they're the same reasons I initially rejected the idea of working with you, too."

"My gut reaction is usually the correct one." He assessed her with one eyebrow raised, then shrugged. "Why force the situation?"

Camilla folded her hands on the table in front of her. "Uncle Lou obviously respects your work and shrewd business sense, or he'd never consider you for this project. This isn't just a random block of properties to him, Kai. He's committed to the revitalization of Southlake Park. It's breaking his heart that he can't finish what he started himself, but..." She halted, averting her gaze.

If Uncle Lou hadn't told Kai why he was selling this property, it certainly wasn't her job to do that.

Kai raised a brow. Her hesitance to state more hadn't gone unnoticed. But he didn't push her on it.

"What about you?" He tipped his bearded chin in her direction. "Do you have that same level of confidence in my

REESE RYAN

ability and *shrewd business sense?*" He repeated her phrase with a slight hint of mockery.

She chose to ignore it. "Yes. I trust that you can build a beautiful, solid home that will add value to the community. And if Uncle Lou says you have a good business head, I believe him. The man knows his stuff."

"But?" He cocked his head, taking another bite of his food, drawing her attention to his tongue.

Her cheeks heated as she met his gaze again. She cleared her throat. "But I don't want this to become another group of homes that obliterates everything that once made them neighborhood jewels. Nor do I want to see them priced out of the range of most residents. As your homes, beautiful though they are, tend to be," she added.

Kai put down his sandwich, wiping his hands on a couple of napkins.

"The homes I build command top dollar because I give people *exactly* what they want. All of the features that are in high demand right now. Open floor plans. High ceilings. Chef-grade appliances. High-end flooring." He ticked each item off on his long, elegant fingers. "And our work is top-notch. We use high-quality materials and never take short-cuts. That's the reputation I've built my career on. I have no intention of changing that now."

"I understand, and there is definitely a place for that, even in Southlake Park. What isn't cool or sustainable for the people of the community is having all of Southlake Park gentrified, one structure at a time. Until there are no homes left for anyone who isn't making at least six-figures." Her tone was soft, pleading. All of her anger and frustration simmered just below the surface.

This conversation called for subtle persuasion and the precision of a scalpel rather than the indiscriminate blud-geoning of an ax.

"That shrewd business sense you and Lou think I have... It's because I run this like a business, not a charity."

"We're not asking for charity, Kai. No, your profit margins won't be as high as they normally are, and you'll be splitting them with me."

His eyes widened in protest. She held up a hand, asking that he allow her to finish first.

"I'm not asking for a fifty-fifty split on this. You'd be putting up most of the capital and taking on the majority of the risk."

"You're not making this collaboration very appealing, Cam." He swigged the last of his juice.

She sighed. Because he was right. She needed to shift the focus of the conversation.

"Kai, I'm so sorry about your dad," she said quietly. Her fingers itching to touch his, so he would understand that she meant every word. But he bawled his hands into fists on the table. His softening gaze suddenly shuttered and his shoulders tensed. He didn't respond.

"I know you brought Arrington Builders to Chicago as a way to restore your family's legacy. And there's probably a part of you that is just as determined to outshine anything your father ever accomplished."

"We knew each other as kids, Camilla. Don't presume to know anything about me now. Especially why I brought my business here." He glanced down at his watch angrily. "Fifteen minutes."

"I'd like to help you honor your father. This community could be a part of that legacy. I propose that we name the community of homes Arrington Village or something like that," she added when one of his brows hiked.

Is he pleasantly surprised or utterly indignant? She couldn't tell for sure.

"We can get a good return on the houses by restoring

them to their former glory, but with a fresh, modern twist. We'll give them high-end finishes, just not top of the line items that would price them out of range. And I have a connection. I can get great appliances, granite, tile and other materials that are top grade but cost a fraction of the price."

He stared at her without speaking before picking up his sandwich and taking the final few bites.

She leaned back against the booth and patiently awaited his response.

"Is that your entire pitch?" His tone was biting.

Camilla's cheeks stung. Kai was enjoying putting her on the hot seat. After their encounter at the town hall meeting, she couldn't blame him.

"I know you haven't lived in Southlake Park for some time. And maybe it doesn't mean anything to you anymore. But it does to me and Uncle Lou. And to folks like Mama Peaches and Ms. Geraldine."

He cut his eyes at her. "That's low, Cam. Even for you."

She let the jab roll off her. *Think of the bigger picture here. You'll have plenty of opportunities to bust his balls once he agrees to the deal.*

"If you don't believe me, talk to Mama Peaches or any of the old folks still left in the neighborhood. Because there aren't a lot of them these days. The community is bleeding residents, leaving boarded-up houses and abandoned buildings in its wake. Making those structures a haven for crime and ripe for the taking for companies who only care about making money. People who don't give a damn about the human carnage caused by their decisions. People like--"

"Arrington Builders," he interrupted, his stare cold. "That's what you were thinking, right? So why don't you just say it?"

"It doesn't have to be that way," she said softly. Her heart thumped loudly in her chest. The sound of it filled her ears.

"Not if you're willing to approach this project the way we're proposing."

"I have to protect my reputation." He jabbed his finger against the table. "And my company's bottom line."

"I'm not asking you to jeopardize either." She leaned forward, elbows on the table. "I'm only asking that you handle the deal with compassion and a sense of responsibility to the old neighborhood."

"Like the compassion the old neighborhood had for me and my brother when my dad got sent up and my mom was sick?" He frowned, his expression racked with pain.

God, she wanted to squeeze his hand. To crawl onto his lap and wrap her arms around him. Tell him that she'd been as heartbroken as he was about both his mother's illness and his father's death. Because despite everything that had happened between their families, she'd once loved the Arringtons as if they were her own flesh and blood.

Regardless of the pain and anger that had been fomented between them because of the awful choices Barris Arrington had made. Or Kai's determination to believe his father's lies rather than accept the painful truth.

His father had been a liar and a thief who'd put both of their families and their livelihoods in jeopardy.

It cost Barris his life and nearly ruined all of theirs.

"Yes," she said quietly. "The same compassion Mama Peaches showed when she stepped up and took you and Keith in so you wouldn't be shipped off to live with your uncle in North Carolina. The same compassion Lou and Dora showed in seeing after you."

"How'd you know--"

"Lou and Dora would never say anything," she assured him. "But one day he'd dropped his checkbook. I was a nosy ass kid." She shrugged. "So I thumbed through it. I saw the duplicates of the checks he'd written Mama Peaches with your name and Keith's in the memo. And the checks he'd sent to your mother."

His frown deepened, and his brows turned downward. And she was sure there was steam coming out of Kai's ears. He rubbed angrily at his chin. "Time's up."

"But I still have another--"

"I've heard enough." His eyes no longer met hers. "The answer is still no."

"Kai, you know this property would be a good investment for your firm." She tried to remain calm.

"I do." His nostrils flared. "But what I don't know is whether or not I can trust you. Trusting an Anthony was the mistake my father made. I'm not inclined to repeat history."

A knot tightened in Camilla's belly as she silently counted backward from ten.

"Look, I know you want to believe your father was a saint. That he was simply a victim in all of this." The anger she felt slowly receded as she saw the pain in his eyes. "But it just isn't true, Kai. Your father put mine in a terrible position. My dad was forced to choose between protecting his best friend with a lie or protecting his family by telling the truth. The choice was clear, though it was painful."

She remembered how distraught her father seemed in the days before Kai's father had been arrested. At the time, she hadn't known why. But she'd since learned that he'd been given the ultimatum of wearing a wire and getting Barris to confess what he'd done or being charged, too. The choice had devastated her father and put his back against the wall.

"It's pointless for us to rehash the past. Neither of our positions is going to change." His dark eyes had gone cold. "It's best if we both just walk away and leave it at that."

"Even if it means walking away from this deal and a chance to reshape your family's legacy here in Southlake Park?"

"Bet," he said. "But the truth is that all I have to do is wait this out. If no one else is willing to meet Uncle Lou's demands, he'll be forced to sell the property *without* stipulations. And when it comes down to it, I know he'd rather that buyer be me than some mega company with no ties to this community. Then I can handle the project however the hell I choose, as it should be."

"That would break his heart. And the last thing Lou needs right now is..." She stopped, wiping at the tears of anger welling in her eyes.

She refused to let Mekkai Arrington see her cry, the way she had when he'd ended their friendship. She would never give him that kind of power again.

"Thanks for your time." Cam stood and turned to leave.

Kai had won this battle. But she wasn't ready to concede the war. She was nowhere close to giving up.

MEKKAI

*K*ai dragged a hand across his forehead as he watched Camilla walk away.

Her angry stride accentuated the sway of her generous hips. He got lost in the fleeting vision of his hands on those hips as he pressed his mouth to hers. Which was exactly why he didn't need to be working closely with Camilla Anthony.

Kai shook his head, hoping to dislodge the image. He tried to massage away the tension at the back of his neck.

Why did Camilla have to push so hard?

She'd made some solid points, but then she made the mistake of bringing up their past. He didn't want or need her pity or the pity of anyone in Southlake Park.

Kai wasn't just furious with Camilla. He was angry with himself for allowing her to get under his skin. For letting her take him back *there*. To those moments when he was an angry teenager who'd seriously considered having *Fuck the World* tattooed across his back.

But he was also angry at himself for being so dismissive of Camilla. He'd once cared deeply for her.

He would always resent Michael Anthony. Still, he'd

matured enough to realize that it wasn't fair of him to lash out at Cam. She didn't deserve to answer for her father's guilt any more than he should be judged for the accusations levied against his.

Guilt churned in his gut remembering how hurt she'd been that day twenty-five years ago. He'd seen a flash of that hurt and pain in her eyes just now.

Don't be an ass, Kai. Apologize for losing your cool.

He glanced toward the door at the sound of screeching tires. Camilla burned rubber out of Hammond Deli's parking lot in a black Mini-Cooper 4-door wagon with a red roof and racing stripes.

An apology would only encourage Cam and further aggravate them both. Why add fuel to a fire he wanted to put out?

Kai scratched at his beard, then dragged a hand through the thick curls piled high atop his head. He checked his watch. He had an hour or so to kill before his next meeting. Just enough time to slide through Kadaris Kuts to see if the owner, Kadaris Kathan, another one of Mama Peaches' Gents, could give him a shave and haircut.

Sexy-ass Camilla Anthony was annoying-as-hell and determined-as-fuck. He needed to clear his head and get his mind off of her. A shave, a fresh haircut, and some time hanging out with the fellas at one of his favorite neighborhood spots was just what he needed.

K ai had learned early on that the neighborhood barbershop was so much more than just a place to get your hair cut. It was a local gathering place for the men in the neighborhood. A place where you could let your guard down and be yourself. Regardless of the problems weighing on you, you left the barbershop feeling better after chopping it up with the fellas.

Sure, they talked shit at the barbershop. But you got called out on that bullshit, if you did. And no one was immune to a good teasing. Not even the owner, Kadaris Kathan.

The guys had been clowning Kadaris hard because not only had Mama Peaches roped him into being a bachelor in the auction, too, but she'd insisted that Kadaris work with Khloe Madison, an old friend turned etiquette coach whom he apparently didn't get along with.

While Kadaris didn't find the ribbing he was getting funny, the customer in his chair certainly did. He'd had to stop three times because the dude was laughing so damn hard that Kadaris almost gashed the top of his head.

"Move like that again, Derrick, and your ass is leaving here with a bald fade," Kadaris warned the client in his chair. "And we all know you ain't got the head for that shit."

"Damn straight. Yo' lumpy rock head would look fucked up with a bald fade. Just look at all them wrinkles on the back of ya neck." Old Mr. Jackson cackled so hard his false teeth shifted.

Kai had never actually seen the old man get a haircut, but he always seemed to be in the shop whenever Kai came for one.

"All right, all right." Derrick sat up straight in his chair, still clutching his belly from laughing so hard. "You ain't got to be so damn sensitive, man."

Kadaris frowned but ignored Derrick's comment. Instead, he shifted the conversation away from himself.

"As usual, y'all are making a big fucking deal out of nothing. I'm not the only gent of Mama Peaches that's doing this auction." Kadaris raised his eyes to meet Kai's momentarily before returning his attention to Derrick's lumpy head. "You tellin' me Mama Peaches didn't recruit you, too, Kai? Or are you over the age limit, old man?" A snide smirk lifted one corner of the man's mouth.

"Oh, I see you got jokes, young blood." Kai shifted in his seat, pointing a finger at Kadaris. "I might be forty, but your ass ain't too far behind me. What are you, thirty-six?"

"Thirty-three." Kadaris chuckled. "Then maybe it's just all that damn gray hair."

"Don't knock it." A grin spread across Kai's face as he stroked his beard, laced with hints of gray, then smoothed the gray hair at his temples. "The ladies love it."

"I know that's right." Mr. Jackson cackled, rubbing a hand over his wooly gray hair. "And I bet it attracts more attention than that tired-ass baseball cap you wear all the damned time, Kadaris."

"Don't worry about me, Mr. J." Kadaris chuckled, turning Derrick in the barber chair so he could access the other side of his head. "I do all right." He lifted his head in Kai's direction. "And don't think I didn't notice that you didn't answer my question."

Kai shifted in his seat, his lips pursed. "Yeah, Mama Peaches shanghaied me, too. I tried to avoid her, but she wasn't having it." He shrugged. "It's the least I can do after everything she's done for me."

"Same here." Kai nodded in agreement. "Though I put up one hell of a fight."

"Damn. Is Mama Peaches that gangsta. Or y'all just a bunch of soft ass muthafuckas who can't say no?" Derrick asked.

"She's that gangsta," the entire shop said nearly in unison, then everyone laughed.

"But seriously, Mama Peaches is an amazing woman," Kai said. "She's done so much for this community and for me, Kadaris, and a bunch of other dudes who might be six feet under right now if it wasn't for her." The other men in the shop nodded fondly. "So there's not much I wouldn't do for her. Hell, I'd walk over hot coals for Mama Peaches."

"Speaking of being raked over hot coals," Mr. J turned his attention to Kai. "I hear Mike Anthony's girl raked your ass over the coals at that town hall meeting the other day." He laughed. "And did it with a smile."

Kai clenched his jaw. "I wouldn't phrase it that way *exactly*."

"Exactly how would you put it?" Kadaris grinned as he adjusted the guards on the clippers. "She took a baseball bat to your dome?"

The entire shop erupted with laughter.

"Camilla Anthony, the lady who refurbishes old houses?" Derrick asked before Kai could respond. The man's eyes glittered with excitement at the mention of Cammie. "Man, that woman is fine as hell. I'd tap that ass for sure."

"Watch your mouth, young blood." Kai's hands balled into fists on his lap and his heart thumped in his chest.

The protective instinct he'd felt toward Camilla when they were kids suddenly kicked in. It took everything in him to remain in that chair rather than flying across the room and grabbing the dude up by the collar.

"My bad, dawg. That you?" Derrick asked.

"No." Kai wasn't inclined to offer the man any further explanation, though he clearly expected one.

"Kai and Cammie were like play cousins back in the day," Kadaris supplied.

"But didn't she just hand you your head on a platter a couple of days ago?" Derrick asked.

"I said they *used* to be play cousins." Kadaris chuckled. But then he shifted an apologetic glance in Kai's direction.

Kadaris, Mr. J, and nearly everyone who'd been longtime

residents of Southlake Park knew about the bad blood between the Arringtons and the Anthonys.

"Why you so damn worried about Cammie Anthony anyway?" Mr. J hiked his wiry, gray brows. "She don't want your little young, ain't got a pot to piss in or a window to throw it out of ass, no way. Camilla Anthony is a grown-ass woman with her own business and several properties. Ain't you still livin' at your mama's house?"

Everyone in the shop erupted into laughter.

"I'm helping her out. You know, while I figure out my next move." Derrick's face flushed.

"Yo! What's S'up, fam?" The little bell above the door jingled, announcing the arrival of Landis Lamberton, Uncle Lou's youngest son. He tipped his chin in greeting as he stepped inside the shop and each man replied with a greeting of his own. "Kadaris, you got time for me today?"

"Five guys ahead of you, and this one won't stop fidgeting," Kadaris met Derrick's eye in the mirror and the other man straightened his spine and sat still. "But yeah, as long as you don't mind the wait."

Landis slid into the chair beside Kai. "What's up, Kai? You'll be at the spot on Saturday, right?" He lowered his voice conspiratorially as he leaned forward.

Kai blinked, staring at the man in silence blankly for a moment before he remembered the invitation he'd received a few weeks ago. "Your birthday party. Right. Friday night at the Renaissance Lounge. Well, I'm not sure..."

"C'mon, man. Don't tell me you're not gonna show. The spot'll be lit. You do *not* want to miss it." Landis jabbed Kai's bicep for emphasis. "We're doing it big, that's why I couldn't invite everyone. You should be glad you made the cut."

Kai forced a smile and sighed, clapping a hand on the man's shoulder. He owed a great debt to Uncle Lou. He wouldn't partner up with Camilla Anthony, but he could at least attend Landis's birthday party. "I'm grateful for the invite, Landis. I'll rearrange my schedule and fly out on Saturday morning instead."

"Going back to North Carolina?" Kadaris asked.

When Kai looked up, everyone in the shop was staring at them. So much for keeping the convo private.

"Just for a few days. I have...stuff to handle back home." Kai shifted in his seat, his neck suddenly hot just thinking about what lay ahead.

"Business or personal?" Landis asked. Everyone in the shop looked at him expectantly.

"Both." He picked up a wrinkled copy of *Sports Illustrated* and held it in front of his face as he turned to a random page and started to read.

"And that's Kai for don't ask me no more damn questions." Mr. J chuckled. The old man climbed to his feet, slipped on his coat, looped a scarf around his neck and pressed his hat on his head. "See y'all young'uns later. Got a date with my ladyfriend in a bit, and it ain't polite to keep her waiting."

"All right then, Mr. J. Check you later," Kadaris nodded toward the older man's retreating back as he exited the shop.

"Whoa!" Kai rubbed a hand over his head as Mr. J climbed inside his 1975 jade green Lincoln Continental Town Coupe with green leather bucket seats. "That bad boy is as clean as it was the day it rolled off the lot."

"It should be. He only drives the thing three places. Here, church on Sunday, and on his weekly date with his ladyfriend, Ms. Maybelline." Kadaris chuckled as he finished lining Derrick up and got a small brush to dust the hair from his shoulders. "Kai, you're up next."

Derrick stood and paid Kadaris for his cut before stepping over to where Landis stood. "Hey man, will Camilla Anthony be at the spot for your birthday?" he asked, his tone hushed.

Landis grinned. "She was one of the first to RSVP."

"Cool. See you then." Derrick gave Landis dap, then put on his jacket and headed into the frigid, blustery wind swirling outside.

Kadaris draped the cape around Kai and secured it behind his neck. He leaned in and spoke quietly, so no one else could hear him. "You alright, man?"

His words shook Kai from his daze. "I'm fine. Why wouldn't I be?" Even Kai recognized how incredibly defensive he sounded. "I was just thinking."

"About Camilla Anthony?" Kadaris shook his head and laughed. "For someone who doesn't like the girl, you sure seem riled up about Derrick's interest in her."

"We're not friends anymore, but that doesn't mean I'm not gonna feel some kind of way about a shady ass dude like Derrick hassling her." Kai kept his voice low, so only Kadaris could hear him.

"He's interested. Maybe too interested," the man conceded. "But I don't know that I'd say he was hassling her."

"Do you honestly think a woman like Camilla would want a guy like Derrick?" Kai turned to look at Kadaris over his shoulder.

"Why? Because he doesn't own his own business like you or me? Or because the plant he worked at got closed and he's in between gigs?" There was censure in the other man's tone. A warning that he was coming off as bougie. Like he thought he was better than the rest of them.

It wasn't true.

"Of course not. I'd like to think you know me better than that." He didn't think he was better than anyone in Southlake Park. But he did think that Camilla was too good for the likes of Derrick. Not because he was down on his luck right now. Because he was an arrogant blowhard. "Derrick is cool enough, but when it comes to women, he's just a cocky boy who wouldn't have a clue how to treat a woman like Camilla."

"*Damn*." Kai let out a low whistle. The corner of his mouth curved in a smirk. "Cam got your head completely fucked up. Thought you said that wasn't you?"

"She doesn't...and she isn't," Kai stammered. "We're not even friends. I just don't want to see some knucklehead like Derrick taking advantage of her."

"If you think she can't fend for herself with a dude like Derrick, then you don't know nothin' about Cam Anthony." Kadaris turned Kai around in his chair. "What are you getting today?"

"Take a little off the top." Kai dragged his fingers through the thick, overgrown curls at his crown. "Line me up and trim my beard." He scratched his chin. "Thanks."

Kai settled in the chair, his attention split between the rapid-fire conversation going on around him and the thoughts swirling in his head—all of which revolved around Camilla Anthony.

CAMILLA

*C*amilla stepped inside the Renaissance Lounge with Letitia Allen, her friend and her assistant at Charming Home Design.

Tish had been a lifesaver, helping her get the paperwork, scheduling, and other essential business factors in line, while freeing her up to spend more time on the creative side of the business. The area in which she excelled.

"The club is popping tonight." Tish surveyed the place as she removed her wrap, revealing a sparkly gold minidress that popped against her dark brown skin and gave her complexion a soft glow under the dim club lights.

"Okay, hot mama." Cammie nudged her friend, pointing a finger at her. "That's how you got those kids in the first place."

"Don't I know it. Wade couldn't resist the power of the pow-pow." Tish placed a hand on each hip as she made the explosive sounds. They both fell out laughing. "Now, let's just hope he can stay up longer than the boys or else they're gonna tear my living room up. He just needs to hold it together until midnight. I promised I'd be home by then."

"I'll be ready to go by then, too." Camilla glanced around the space, her head bopping to the verses J. Cole was laying down on the latest joint by Miguel.

Cam had left the partying behind in her late twenties. Now she was just as happy cozied up on her couch watching a romantic comedy or one of her favorite Marvel movies for the fortieth time.

"Still, I'm glad we drove separately." Tish spoke loudly enough to be heard over the sound of the blaring music. "Because we ain't been here ten damn minutes and already a fine black king has set his sights on you."

Tish tipped her head, indicating that Cammie should look up.

She did, her eyes widening with surprise when she met the man's warm, liquid gaze. Heat shot down her spine. Her nipples and the space between her thighs warmed and tingled.

Cammie acknowledged him with a tip of her chin and a polite smile before quickly dropping her gaze. "That's just Kai."

"Wait. That fine brotha is Mekkai Arrington? My God, no wonder you want to work with him."

"Careful there, lady." Cammie chuckled. "You're a happily married woman, remember?"

"But my eyes still work. Both of them. So I can see how fine that dude is and how he was checking you out from head-to-toe the moment we stepped inside the door." Tish half-shouted over the music as they made their way to the stairs which led to the upper VIP floor. "If you ask me, he was camped out in that spot, waiting for you to get here."

Cam glanced at the spot where Kai had been standing with a tumbler in hand, but he was gone. If Tish hadn't seen him, too, she might've chalked it up to her imagination. Because she'd been thinking about Kai a lot lately.

That reality didn't sit well with her. She wasn't a tween with a crush on the cute boy who was four years older than her. And she wasn't looking for a relationship. She needed a business partner. Thoughts of Kai in any other capacity were a dangerous exercise that would only leave her hurt and disappointed.

"He hates me." It was a reminder to herself as much as it was a warning to her friend to just let it go. "So I assure you that he wasn't waiting for me to arrive. But now that I'm here, there's a good chance he'll leave."

She'd wondered if Kai would be at Landis's birthday party. Part of her half hoped he would be. She wanted another shot at convincing him to collaborate on the project.

"How long have you been divorced?" Tish asked.

"Five years."

"You've been out of the game too long. Maybe that's why you don't recognize the look of desire in a man's eyes. Because that's what I saw in that man's face. Yeah, he might still be mad about all that stuff between y'all's daddies. But that man wants you. And I'm not just talking business, if you know what I mean." She lifted her brows up and down.

Cam couldn't help laughing. "You know that's creepy, right?"

Tish did it again, causing them both to dissolve into laughter.

A gorgeous young woman with a slick ponytail and an ultra-short skirt checked for their names on her clipboard before allowing them to step behind the velvet rope.

"Cam, I'm so glad you made it." Landis enveloped her in a bear hug, then stepped back and held her at arm's length. "Damn girl, you look good tonight. I know it's killing you to be out of your leggings and jeans for a change."

"You know me too well, Landis." Cam laughed as she held

up a silver iridescent gift bag. "This is for you. Happy birthday."

He kissed her cheek. "Thanks, Cam. I know I'm gonna love it. You give the best gifts." He winked. "You lovely ladies help yourselves. The appetizers are over there, and the first two drinks are on the house."

He disappeared to put his gift on a table piled with them.

Tish jabbed her in the side with her elbow.

"Ouch!" Cammie complained. "Did you sharpen those bony elbows in the pencil sharpener before you came out tonight?"

"Fine ass brotha at two o'clock. He's been staring since Landis gave you that hug." Tish at least had the decency to lean in and whisper loudly in her ear rather than shouting like she had before.

Cam glanced over in the direction that Tish indicated, but either her friend was teasing her, or Kai had already gone.

"Are you sure you're not seeing things?" Cam teased. "If you are, it's kind of early. We haven't even had our first drink yet."

"He was there, I'm telling you."

"Fine." Cam waved a hand, as if it didn't matter either way. "Let's grab a drink."

They jostled for space at the bar and finally got the bartender's attention.

"A dirty martini for me, extra dirty and lots of olives," Cammie practically shouted at the man. "And for my friend..." She turned to Tish.

"A virgin strawberry daiquiri."

Cammie began to repeat her friend's request, when suddenly the words struck her. "Wait, you don't at least want a glass of wine?"

After repeating her request to the bartender so he could begin their order, a goofy smile spread across Tish's face and she placed a hand on her belly. "I'd love a glass of wine, but I don't think it would be very good for the baby."

Cam's eyes dropped to the woman's belly. She'd noticed a small bulge there and the slight widening of her friend's hips. But she'd attributed it to her love of soul food, home-made baked goods and premium ice cream. Cam hadn't mentioned it because she didn't want to make her friend self-conscious.

"You're pregnant? How? I mean...how far along are you?"

"Four months beginning today." Tish held up four fingers. "We didn't want to say anything until we were officially in our second trimester. Besides, you're my boss, so I wasn't sure how glad you'd be to hear that I'll be taking maternity leave in about six months."

"We'll find someone to fill in for you *temporarily*," Cam emphasized the word. "And you're not just my assistant, Tish. You're my friend. I know how much you and Wade want a little girl. So of course, I'm happy for you."

"Thanks, Cam." Tish hugged her.

Camilla really was happy for Tish. Just as she was happy for her friend and former college roommate, Rhonda Rice, who lived in California with her growing brood of adorable boys who were little carbon copies of their handsome father. Rhonda was pregnant and hoping for a little girl this time, too.

But what she would never admit to Rhonda, Tish, or her mother—who constantly implored her to get remarried and give her more grandbabies—is that a tiny piece of her was envious of them.

They'd each found the love of their life and were happily raising a family together. She hadn't completely given up hope that she'd eventually meet and marry Mr. Right. But it was becoming less likely that she'd do so while she could still have children of her own.

For now, she'd have to be satisfied with being the cool aunt to her brother's and Rhonda's children.

Camilla wasn't prepared to give up the work that she loved. And maybe her ex-husband was right, she couldn't have it all. But maybe one day, she could have a little of both.

She finally released Tish from her tight hug.

"Everything okay, boss?" Tish eyed her sympathetically.

Great. Now she was garnering the woman's pity.

"Everything is fantastic." Camilla stuffed a tip in the man's overflowing tip jar and retrieved their drinks from the bar. She handed Tish her virgin strawberry daiquiri and raised her own glass. "Tonight, in addition to Landis's birthday, we're celebrating your happy news."

"Thanks, Cam." Tish squeezed her arm. "You're the best boss-slash-friend I could ever ask for."

They clinked their glasses and sipped their drinks.

Cam caught a glimpse of Kai walking by, embroiled in a deep conversation with Landis's older brother Lou Jr., who everyone called LJ.

Kai looked incredibly handsome with his fresh haircut. He wore a black sweater, which looked like cashmere, over slim, gray pants. The black leather boots he wore were more dressy than casual. And something about his distinctive walk and the gray streaks in his temples and freshly-trimmed beard were so damn sexy she felt the need to cross her legs.

"Maybe next time go with a padded bra." Tish sipped her drink, nodding toward Cam's chest.

Cam glanced down at her nipples, visible through the clingy material of her backless, black, bodycon jumpsuit.

"But it's pretty dark in here. Maybe Tall, Dark and Handsome won't notice your headlights." One corner of Tish's mouth rose in a smirk as she took another sip of her drink.

Cam's cheeks stung and she folded her arms, hoping no

one else noticed. Kai seemed determined to avoid her tonight, so at least she wouldn't have the humiliation of him knowing exactly how he affected her.

MEKKAI

*K*ai studied Camilla from across the room as she laughed with her friend over drinks. She looked amazing in a black jumpsuit that hugged every single curve on her incredibly sexy body. And while he'd been impressed enough with the garment when he'd seen her arrive earlier that evening, he was completely mesmerized when she turned her back toward him and whispered something to her friend.

Damn!

The jumpsuit was backless, with a large bow at the back of her neck. The cutout in back showcased her smooth brown skin and stopped just above her peach-shaped bottom.

His heart thumped so loudly in his chest that the sound filled his ears and his pulse raced.

Was it his imagination, or was this woman getting finer every time he saw her? Cam raked her manicured nails through her big, sexy mane of shiny, corkscrew curls. When she shook her head, the curls swung and bounced.

Kai's fingers curled around his glass of Crown Royal XO on the rocks.

LJ, Uncle Lou's oldest son cleared his throat, then chuckled when he finally drew Kai's attention.

For a moment, he'd forgotten LJ was there.

"You alright, man?" his friend asked.

"Why wouldn't I be?" Kai's cheeks heated, embarrassed that he'd been caught shamelessly checking Camilla out. "And don't try to change the subject. I need you to reason with your dad, LJ."

"Look man, I feel your pain. I honestly do. And I know you're not accustomed to working that way." LJ, who looked so much like Uncle Lou as a much younger man, took a sip of his drink. "But my dad and I have one hard and fast rule. He doesn't interfere in my business, and I don't interfere in his. So I'm sorry, brother, but you're on your own on this one."

"C'mon, LJ. I need your help, man. Couldn't you make an exception just this once?"

"Hell no." LJ laughed. "That's a precedent I don't want to set. Besides, let's keep it one-hundred, man. Camilla is damn good at what she does. She's won dozens of awards, and she's been a guest on local morning shows and national home improvement shows. Cam is making a name for herself and Charming Home Design."

Kai groaned and took another sip of his drink. He glanced toward the spot on the dance floor where Cam and her friend were dancing gleefully.

"Does she know?" LJ nodded in Cammie's direction.

"That I don't want to collaborate with her on this? Yes. I've been clear and consistent about my decision since your dad suggested it." Kai took another sip from his glass.

"Not what I meant." LJ grinned. "I mean does Cammie have any idea that you have a thing for her?"

Heat spread through Kai's face, and he coughed, nearly choking on his premium whisky.

"That's crazy," Kai sputtered as LJ slapped him on the back unnecessarily hard a few times. "I don't have a thing for—"

"Save it, bruh." LJ held up a hand. "I've been watching you sneak glances at her since she arrived. Except for when you're openly staring at her, like you were just now." LJ shook the ice in his nearly empty glass. "Is that the *real* reason you don't want to work with her? I know that when we were kids we were always taught to keep our hands off Cam and treat her like a sister. But that was more than twenty years ago." LJ smacked Kai's stomach with the back of his hand, taking him by surprise. "Pretty sure the statute of limitations on that one has run its course. If you're interested in Cam, tell her. You know she's always had a big crush on you." LJ shrugged. "Maybe there's still something there for her, too."

"I hope you don't rely on gossip and conspiracy theories when you're defending your clients, *Mr. Defense Attorney*." Kai sipped the last of his whisky.

"Never. But I am dogged about getting to the truth. Which is what I'm doing now. You should try it. It'll set you free." LJ chuckled. "Pun intended." He set his glass down. "Time for me to call it a night. Tomorrow morning, I'm prepping a client for trial next week. So in closing, no I can't help you with your little dilemma with my dad. And yes, you should tell Cam that you're interested. The worst she can do is tell you to drop dead."

"You were zero help, LJ," Kai grumbled. I hope your client fares better."

LJ laughed, slapping palms with Kai and tugging him forward into a one-arm hug. "Love you, too, man."

Kai got the attention of one of the servers and requested

another drink. And though he tried not to, he found himself scanning the room in search of Cam. She and her friend in the gold dress were out on the floor dancing.

He chastised himself for watching her again, but he couldn't help it. Camilla Anthony swaying her generous hips on the dance floor was just about the sexiest thing he'd ever seen.

CAMILLA

*C*amilla and Tish had hit the dance floor together, not waiting for anyone to ask either of them to dance. But then there was a tap on her shoulder. Cam turned around.

It was Landis, and he was completely lit. He'd definitely had more than his two complimentary drinks.

"Care to dance, beautiful?" he slurred, his tone more flirtatious than she could recall it ever being.

"How can I turn down the birthday boy?" Cam smiled. "Do you mind, Tish?"

"Girl, no." Tish seemed relieved. "I know these shoes look good, but my damn dogs are barking. I'm gonna sit over there and check in with Wade and the boys."

The heavy bass faded, and a slower song came on. Landis grinned. "Perfect timing."

For him maybe.

He took her in his arms, his grin turning into more of a smirk.

She smiled politely and tried to relax in his arms, despite

the fact that they were only a few hours into the festivities, and he smelled like he'd fallen into a vat of Grey Goose.

"It's a great party. Thank you for inviting me and for allowing me to bring Tish," she said finally.

"Is Tish your date? No judgement." He shrugged. "In fact, it was kind of hot watching you two out on the dance floor."

"You're an idiot, and you're drunk," she said, her tone teasing. "Did you forget I was married to a man for five years?"

He gave her an *is-that-supposed-to-mean-something?* shrug. She sighed and shook her head.

"Tish is married with two kids and another on the way. And I'm definitely on Team Vitamin D. At least for now. This conversation is making me rethink my choice."

"Sorry. I'm a little drunk, but you probably already know that." He laughed so hard he snorted.

Cammie shook her head, but couldn't help laughing, too. "After this dance, you need to sit your ass down somewhere with a cup of coffee or three. Otherwise, you'll pass out in a corner, sucking your thumb, and miss out on the rest of your party."

"Hey, I stopped sucking my thumb when I was five."

"It was closer to seven, but whatever," she chuckled. "The point is, take it easy and slow down. Puking at your own party is not cool. Or did you forget that from last year. And the year before."

"Okay, you're right. I'll go get some coffee when this song is done."

"Brilliant idea." She poked him in the gut.

When the song ended, Landis headed toward the bar to order coffee and she turned to join Tish on the couch. Her friend was having an animated conversation on her cellphone. Tish frowned deeply. Her brows gathered as she kneaded the back of her neck.

Cam was headed toward her friend when suddenly someone grabbed her hand. She turned around quickly.

Derrick Moseley. The one man she'd been hoping *not* to see.

"What's up, Cam? Been looking for you all night." He rubbed his chin and studied her like a butcher trying to decide which cut of meat he was going to start with.

"I've been here for the past three hours." She forced a polite smile. "And this is my first time seeing you."

A grin spread across his face. "So you were looking for me."

Not what I said. She sighed.

Derrick wasn't an awful person, but he was several years younger than she was, and they had nothing in common. He was deeply interested in her, while she had zero interest in him.

Cam was a fairly direct person, as she'd been with Landis. But Derrick had run into a string of bad luck, and she felt sorry for him. So she'd been handling him with kid gloves by giving him subtle hints that she wasn't interested.

The hints had obviously been too subtle.

"I was just going to check on my friend. But it was good seeing you, Derrick." She turned to walk away, but he slipped his hand into the crook of her elbow.

He leaned close to her ear so she could hear him amidst all the noise. "I walked all the way over here to ask you to dance, Cam. You not gon' leave me hangin', are you? The fellas will never stop riding me over this, if you do."

In her head, she knew all the reasons she was in no way obligated to help Derrick save face with his boys. But when she studied his pitiful, puppy dog eyes, she sighed.

She glanced over at Tish again. She seemed calmer. Maybe everything was fine now. "One dance, then I need to check on my friend."

She turned toward Derrick but didn't make an effort to close the space between them.

Derrick gave her a knowing grin and stepped closer, leaving a small space between them. He slipped his hands around her waist.

They moved to the music in silence as Cam glanced over to the bar where Landis was drinking his coffee and flirting with a female bartender. Then she glanced around the dance floor, studying some of the other couples.

She looked anywhere but at Derrick as he tried his best to engage her in meaningless small talk. Camilla was polite, but distant, as she always was with Derrick. His grandmother was a sweet, older woman who'd been one of her favorite neighbors growing up. So the kid gloves she was using with Derrick were as much a reflection of her affection for the old woman as they were in deference to the younger man's current situation.

But respect and pity only went so far.

"Cam, I need to go." Tish appeared suddenly, digging in her purse. "The boys are sick, and Wade is freaking out."

"I'm so sorry, hon. No worries, we can leave now--"

"No need to ruin your night." Tish flashed a smile in Derrick's direction. "This is exactly why I insisted that we drive separately. I'll text you once I get home." Tish wiggled her eyebrows. "And try not to have too much fun."

Her friend had turned on her skinny gold heels and disappeared into the crowd in an instant, leaving Cam standing there motionless, with her mouth hanging open.

Derrick started swaying to the music again and she followed him. She even danced with him to the next two songs, which thankfully were much faster.

When the third song ended, Cam thanked Derrick for the dance and excused herself to go check on Landis. But as she turned to leave, he slipped his hand in hers and leaned down, his lips pressed to her ear, so she could hear him above the thumping bass "You're a smart, beautiful woman, Cam. So you have to know I'm feeling you. If you gave me a legit shot at this, I think you'd be feeling me, too."

"Look, Derrick, it's like I told you before--"

"You're not looking for a relationship right now." He echoed the words she'd said previously. "Maybe that's just because you haven't found the right dude. Or maybe you have, and you just don't realize it yet."

Cam raised her eyes to his soft, pleading ones. And there it was again. She felt sorry for him and didn't want to bruise his ego any further. But she had to put an end to this. *Now.* Leaving him no doubt that this wasn't going to happen. Ever.

Even if she had to tell a little white lie to do it.

"You're right. I did just need to find the right guy. And I have. I'm involved with someone, and things have gotten pretty serious between us. So..." She tugged her arm free and took a step away from him.

Derrick rubbed a hand over his head, his expression had transformed from a soft plea to a wounded scowl.

"But I've been trying to get with you for a minute, and you never mentioned having a dude." His tone was indignant and his jaw tight. He actually looked angry. As if she'd owed him first dibs.

Cam wasn't afraid. She was *pissed.*

She'd gone out of her way to be kind to Derrick's sad sack, down-on-his-luck ass. And he was really going to stand here and act like she owed him an explanation?

Oh, hell nawl.

Cammie raised one hand, to point it in his face and tell this mofo about his damn self when someone grabbed her hand. Something she was getting sick and tired of tonight.

She turned to read the perpetrator the riot act, but she

was stunned to see the one man who'd been actively avoiding her all night. "Kai?"

"Dance with me." It was more of a directive than a question. His eyes locked with hers.

Her first instinct was to object. She didn't need Kai Arrington fighting her battles. She was a grown-ass woman, fully capable of handling this entitled blowhard on her own.

But there was something about Kai's expression. The one that pleaded with her to just roll with it rather than causing a fuss.

She heaved a sigh, acknowledging his request with the slight tip of her chin, before turning to Derrick and thanking him again for the dance.

The younger man's nostrils flared. He glared at her, then at Kai, whose expression communicated a clear don't-try-me-son-or-I-will-fuck-you-up vibe. If she hadn't been so annoyed with both of them for their public dick-measuring contest, she would've laughed.

Derrick turned and stormed off the dance floor.

Kai leaned down so she could hear him. "You're welcome."

"I was just about to handle him," she replied quickly, still fired up. She heaved a sigh, then added, "But thank you."

He stared down at her, his hands shoved in his pockets. Neither of them moved, despite everyone dancing frantically around them.

"I'll talk to Derrick. Tell him to back the fuck up, in no uncertain terms." He huffed. "I checked him the other day, but I see he didn't get the message. Shoulda laid my hands on his disrespectful ass then."

"You talked to Derrick about me? Why? When?" The questions escaped her mouth in rapid succession.

"*Yes.*" It seemed to pain him to admit that. "Because I didn't like how he was talking about you. Earlier this week at

Kadaris's shop." He answered her questions in the same order in which she'd posed them.

"Look, I appreciate you looking out for me, Kai. But I don't need a big brother. What I need is a business partner."

"C'mon Cam, don't start that again. This is Landis's birthday party. Don't you ever turn that brain of yours off?"

"No," she responded without hesitation. "Turning off my brain is how I ended up with my loser ex-husband," she muttered under her breath.

"What?" He practically shouted over the music.

"Nothing." She dragged a hand through her curls in frustration before raising her gaze to his. "You spent all night ignoring me. So why would you suddenly ride in like Shaft, guns blazing, to rescue me from Derrick?"

Kai shifted his gaze, staring over her shoulder before his eyes returned to hers. "Dance with me," he said again. His tone was softer, and his warm stare conveyed more of a plea than a demand.

Her belly fluttered and the flippant response she'd intended to make died on her tongue.

Camilla released a quiet sigh and stepped forward, allowing Kai to slip his long arms around her waist and pull her closer to him as they swayed to the music.

Cam wrapped her arms around his back, one palm pressed to his soft, black cashmere sweater. She got a whiff of his cologne. A luscious scent that made her wonder inappropriate things...like how long the scent would linger on her pillow.

They moved together in silence, warmth dancing along her spine and heat building in her core in response to the heavenly sensation of Kai holding her in his arms, his large hand pressed to her bare back.

They danced to a few more songs together. Another slow one, then a couple of faster songs with a hard, driving beat.

There was something so incredibly sexy about the way he danced. And about the way their bodies moved together.

But the last thing she needed was to fuel the fire. Thoughts of Kai Arrington already filled her head during the day. And he starred in the vivid, naughty dreams she awoke from in the middle of the night.

When the song ended, she dropped her arms and stepped back. "It's getting late and my friend already left. I'd better head home, too. Goodnight, Kai."

"Wait, I have an early flight. I'll walk you out."

After they'd said their goodbyes to Landis, they walked out to the parking lot in near silence.

Cam tossed her clutch inside her MINI Cooper Clubman and shut the door again. She leaned against the outside of the car with her arms folded and studied his handsome face in the glow of the light overhead. "There's obviously something you want to say to me."

Kai rubbed his chin and heaved a sigh as he stepped forward. He left just a sliver of space between them.

"I need to tell you I'm sorry about how I behaved at Hammond's Deli the other day. My mother raised me better than that. So did Mama Peaches. They'd both be ashamed of how short I was with you. You didn't deserve that, and I'm sorry."

Cam stared at him, at a complete loss for words.

Yep, this was all definitely just a dream.

MEKKAI

*K*ai stood just a few inches from Cammie, her sweet scent reminiscent of a field of flowers, with hints of citrus. The scent tickled his nose but wasn't overpowering.

She stared at him, her big brown eyes blinking, as if she couldn't believe what she heard.

Great. She believed that he was such an ill-mannered miscreant that he was incapable of a basic human decency like offering a well-deserved apology. But on the upside, she was completely silent. Something that might never happen again. Which meant that he should take advantage of this opportunity to get out everything he needed to say to her.

"And I need to apologize for how I treated you that day… back then. I was a hotheaded kid, and my entire life had just imploded. I was angry. Ready to blame anyone and everyone. I took it out on you. Blamed your entire family for what your father did." He dragged his fingers through the curls at the crown of his head. "You were just trying to be a friend and I..." He sighed. "I couldn't see past my own pain and anger."

"I don't know what to say," she finally stammered, her

eyes searching his. "I get how hurt and angry you must've been. That's why I came to see you that day. I just wanted to...I don't know. Help, I guess."

He nodded, the memory of his behavior that day pained him. "I realize that now, but at the time, the last thing I wanted was help from anyone with the last name Anthony."

She frowned, her brows furrowing. "My dad did what he had to do, Kai. He's not your adversary. My family prayed for yours every night. And we worried about you every day. We made every effort to reach out--"

"I know, and I don't want to rehash who's wrong and who's right again. Neither of our positions have changed on that. But I also need you to know that my position on us working together hasn't changed either."

She folded her arms and frowned. "I see."

Kai noticed movement across the parking lot.

"Derrick." He gritted his teeth, indicating where the man stood with a tilt of his head. He was watching them, probably waiting to talk to Cammie again. "This dude is having one hell of a time taking no for an answer. I'm going to talk to him now."

Cammie grabbed his arm. "I don't need you to fight my battles, Kai. Besides, I told Derrick that I'm with someone else now. After you stepped in earlier, he probably thinks that's you."

Kai swiped a hand across his forehead. *The barbershop. Shit.*

"He probably would've, but he asked me flat-out if we were together and I said we weren't."

"Why would he ask you about me? Is this what you guys do at the barbershop, gossip like a bunch of old hens?" She propped her fist on one cocked hip.

"Yes, it's what men do at the barbershop. And I'm not the one who brought you up. Derrick did. I'm the one who defended you. Why am I not getting any credit for that?"

Camilla glanced over toward where he'd seen Derrick standing, her arms folded as she drummed her fingers. Suddenly, she froze, her eyes meeting his for a moment.

"Don't freak, Kai." Her voice was low as she reached out and grabbed the lapels of his coat, tugging him toward her until there was hardly any space left between them. "But I'm going to kiss you. Not for real. Just enough for Derrick to get the—"

Before she finished her sentence, Kai lowered his head and pressed his lips to hers. His arms glided around her waist as he kissed the creamy, dusty rose, gloss off her full lips.

She'd initially gasped in surprise, her body stiffening beneath his. But as he slipped his hands beneath her wool coat, pressing his fingertips to her back, she started to relax. To meld against him, her lips parting.

This was meant to be an act. A show to make Derrick believe he'd lied at that barbershop when he'd said that he and Camilla weren't together. But nothing about this *felt* like an act. It felt very real and yet, a little bit like a dream. Because he'd imagined what it would be like to kiss Camilla every day since they'd crossed paths at that town hall meeting.

Camilla looped her arms around his neck, pulling him toward her. Her kiss was hungry. Eager. But there was something soft and tender about it, too.

Kai slipped his tongue between her parted lips. Could taste the salty remnants of the martinis she'd consumed earlier. His tongue glided against hers and he slid his hands down her back and over her ass, as firm and ripe as a Georgia peach in June.

Her back pressed against the cold, hard exterior of her

car as her lower body strained toward his, eager for the contact between them.

His heart pounded in his chest and his body filled with heat, his growing desire for her pressed between them. All thoughts about Derrick had faded from his brain. He was only thinking of Camilla. Of how much he wanted her and all the reasons he shouldn't.

Finally, he pulled his mouth from hers, both of them panting. Their breath created little puffs of smoke in the frigid night air, visible beneath the glow of the street light.

They stared at each other for a moment in silence. Then they both blurted, "I'm sorry," simultaneously.

"I shouldn't have put you on the spot like that," Cam said quickly, lowering her gaze to his shoulder as she folded her arms again. "I didn't even ask if you're already involved with someone."

"I'm not. I wouldn't have kissed you, if I was. I'm not that guy." He rubbed at the back of his neck. "But I'm also not prepared to get involved right now."

"Oh, God no. Me neither. I wasn't asking because I'm interested. I've got too much on my plate to even consider a relationship. I just don't want to put anything you might have going on in jeopardy. That's all."

"You didn't."

"Good." Cam reached in her pocket and pulled out a silk-lined knit hat. She slipped it on, tucking a few stray curls beneath it while allowing the rest to hang out of the back. She glanced around the lot. "Derrick's gone, but his car is still there. I guess he went back inside the club."

Kai searched the parking lot and nodded. "I guess he did. But I should follow you home, just the same."

A faint smile curved one corner of her mouth. "That's sweet, Kai. But I'll be fine."

She opened her door, slipped behind the steering wheel,

and started her car. "And don't think I've given up on the idea of working together. I know you don't see it yet, but this is an amazing opportunity for both of us. And maybe it's a chance to repair our friendship, too."

He raised his collar and shoved his hands in his coat pockets. A chill ran through him now that he no longer had her body heat to warm him. Two decades of living in the South had made him soft. His body still hadn't adjusted to the brisk Chicago weather.

"Let me ask you a question, Cam."

"Shoot."

"What do your parents think about us collaborating on this project?"

She shifted her gaze from his and pulled her coat tightly around her. "I've been busy, so I haven't had a chance to talk to them about it, yet. But I will when I have dinner with them on Sunday."

One corner of his mouth lifted in a smirk. "If you get your parents' blessing on the deal, I'll consider it."

The disappointment on her face told him everything he needed to know.

"Goodnight, Cam." He closed her car door and stepped back, watching as she pulled out of her parking space and drove off.

It was the reminder he needed to pull him back to reality. He was glad he'd apologized. He was even glad that there might be a chance of him and Cammie resuming some semblance of a friendship. But a relationship—business or otherwise—was simply out of the question.

His life was already complicated enough.

MEKKAI

*K*ai stepped out of his truck and inhaled the salty ocean breeze that had become so familiar. Pleasure Cove had become home as much as Southlake Park was. And on a glorious, late-March morning when the temperature was easily thirty degrees warmer than the frigid air he'd left behind in Chicago, he missed it.

Kai headed up the path to his mother's little cottage. The little clapboard structure, painted Robin's egg blue and trimmed in white, sat just off the beach in Pleasure Cove. It had been his first solo renovation project and a gift to his mother.

Kai knocked on the wooden screen door—an original feature of the house his mother had insisted on keeping—rather than ringing the bell. The smell of bacon wafted through the open door.

"I'm coming!" A familiar voice called from a distance. Finally, his mother peeked her head through the doorway of the kitchen. "Kai? Honey, you didn't tell me you were coming home this weekend."

She rushed to the door, unlocking it and giving him a bear hug.

He sighed. His entire body relaxed as he hugged his mother back.

"You look great, Ma. But then, you always do." He grinned as he released her.

His mother was nearly sixty-five, but her tawny brown skin was smooth and beautiful. And her mostly white hair was cut in a cute, contemporary style that showed off her gorgeous face. She wore a crisp, white button-down shirt and a pair of light denim capris.

"Thank you, baby." She smiled, heading back toward the kitchen as he trailed her. "I see you got a fresh cut before you came home. It looks good, and so does the beard. Makes you look very distinguished."

"Thanks." He stroked his beard without thought. "How is everything going?"

"I'm doing well, honey. Really," she assured him. "There's no need for you to worry. I'm fine. It's my job to worry about you. Not the other way around. So tell me, how are things going for you in Chicago?"

"Good." He shrugged, taking a seat at a barstool on the other side of the island. "Arrington Builders has been taking on a steady stream of jobs, and we're getting rave reviews."

"But?" His mother started lining up strips of bacon on the griddle, without even asking. She knew him well enough to know he hadn't eaten yet.

"We're making headway in some of the hottest neighborhoods in the Chicagoland area, including our old neighborhood." He paused, taking in his mother's reaction.

She froze, her posture stiff. His mother sucked in a slow, deep breath before resuming her task.

"That's wonderful dear. But you still haven't gotten to the

but." She turned the fire on beneath the griddle and turned to face him as she washed her hands at the sink.

"The one neighborhood I'm still having trouble breaking into is Southlake Park."

"Southlake Park isn't the only neighborhood in Chicago, you know, Kai." Her tone was soft, and her gaze was reassuring.

"I know. And it shouldn't be so important for me to build there, but—"

"It is." Lana Arrington forced a smile. "The heart wants what the heart wants. Even when our heads know better." She sighed softly, and for a moment it was clear her thoughts had drifted off elsewhere.

His mother shut off the water and dried her hands on a towel before returning it to its hook. "What's the barrier that's holding you back."

Kai swallowed hard and sighed, raising his eyes to hers. "Camilla Anthony."

His mother's eyes widened with surprise. "Little Cammie?" She pulled a glass measuring cup filled with pancake mix from the refrigerator and removed the foil covering it. "What's Cammie got to do with whether or not you can build in Southlake Park?"

As his mother made pancakes, Kai recounted Camilla's objections to his planned community in Southlake Park, including her speech at the town hall meeting that effectively killed the deal.

"She must be about…thirty-six," his mother mused. "What does she look like now?"

Kai pulled his phone from his pocket and pulled up the About page on Charming Home Design's website. He'd studied the site, the company's portfolio, and watched several of her interviews and appearances on local morning shows and a national renovation network. He enlarged

Cam's photo and turned the phone toward his mother as she set the plate of steaming hot pancakes and crispy bacon in front of him.

His mother pressed her fingertips to her mouth. She took the phone from him, her eyes teary as she studied the photo. A soft smile caused her eyes to crinkle at the damp corners. "My God, she's gorgeous. And look at all of that thick, curly hair. She looks so much like her mother, but I can see a lot of her dad in her, too."

She handed the phone back and climbed onto the stool beside him as he ate.

He didn't comment on how gorgeous the string bean little girl with buckteeth and impossibly long legs had turned out. But by his mother's smirk, she'd obviously taken his silence as agreement.

"I know there's a lot of bad history between our family's, but you two were once friends," his mother reminded him. As if he could ever have forgotten. "You wouldn't let anyone lay a finger on her and she practically worshipped you. Perhaps if the two of you just sat down and talked," she suggested.

"We talked after the town hall meeting, Ma. Cam wouldn't budge. Not that it mattered by then."

"She always was a fiery, passionate little thing. Going to bat for the underdog. Saving stray kittens and birds with broken wings." A faint smile kissed his mother's lips as she fiddled with the diamond necklace around her neck. A gift from his father after his birth. She rarely took off the necklace or the tennis bracelet his father had given her after the birth of his younger brother, Keith. "I doubt that she's intentionally trying to sabotage your plans."

"That's her story." He shrugged, nibbling on a strip of crisp bacon. "Apparently, she's been battling the gentrification of Southlake Park since long before I returned to town. Not that that's what I'm doing."

"Of course not, honey." His mother placed a warm hand on his arm. "But from her perspective…" His mother gave him an apologetic smile. "You're not building cozy little homes like this one there. It's all top of the line, super modern, high-end finishes—"

"You're taking her side?"

"I'm always on your side, honey. You know that." She pressed a hand to his cheek and smiled. "But I think it would help if you understood where Cammie and anyone else in the community who might feel the same is coming from, that's all. Coffee?"

"Please." He ate more of the fluffy, delicious blueberry pancakes and finished the last of his bacon. "And after all of the trouble Cam has caused me, Uncle Lou actually suggested that she and I work together on a reno project."

"In Southlake Park?" His mother raised a brow as she poured him a cup of hot, black coffee. He nodded. "What would make Lou suggest that you and Cammie work together?"

"He trusts my craftsmanship and business sense. But he trusts her to ensure that the aesthetic of the homes stays true to the neighborhood and that they won't be priced out of range."

"Sounds like a good plan." His mother folded her arms, "You don't agree?"

"She sank my project, Ma." He gripped his coffee cup. "And she's been fighting me at every turn. Why should I trust her?"

"What did she say when you two talked?" Lana ignored his question.

"That it isn't personal, and she's glad I'm doing so well. She claims that her only objective is to protect the neighborhood and ensure that there's affordable housing for the residents."

"See?" His mother smiled triumphantly, taking the griddle to the sink and cleaning it. "And what does she think about the two of you partnering up?"

"She thinks it's a great idea." Kai walked his plate over to the sink and washed the syrup from his hands. "I've turned her down two or three times already. She still hasn't taken the hint."

His mother laughed. A joyful, melodious sound that he'd learned to treasure after his father's troubles and his mother's illness. It'd been years before she laughed again after his father's death.

"Cammie hasn't changed much, then?" His mother wiped tears from her eyes, still laughing. "I'm telling you, that little girl was so determined. She always knew exactly what she wanted. Back then, that was you."

His mother laughed even harder at his expression in response to her words.

"Cam was a kid with a crush," he said quickly.

"She certainly isn't a little kid now. Is she married?"

"Divorced, from what I hear." Kai dried his hands on a kitchen towel. "Why does that matter?"

"Maybe this is like when she was a little girl and she really just wanted your attention," she suggested, her eyes filled with hope.

"She's not looking for a relationship, and neither am I. Besides, my life is complicated enough as it is. Until I know where things stand with—"

"I know." His mother placed a hand on his. "Either way, everything will work out. I promise."

He heaved a sigh of frustration and rubbed the knot of tension that suddenly arose in his neck as he sank onto the barstool again. He didn't want to think about his stupid mistake or the possible consequences of it. Not until he had to.

"How do you know Cammie isn't looking for a relationship?" The corner of his mother's mouth curved with an expectant smile.

"What?" It was purely a stall tactic. He clearly understood what she'd deduced and was implying.

Lana Arrington poked a finger in his chest and laughed. "And now you're stalling. There is definitely something you're not telling me about this thing with you and Cammie."

"There is no *thing* with me and Cam. And I don't want to talk about her anymore. Okay? I see her in my dreams as it is." His mother's eyes widened. *"Nightmares.* I meant to say that I see her in my nightmares, as it is."

"So since you two talked relationships," his mother continued, barreling past his request to drop the topic of Camilla Anthony. "Did you tell her about your...situation?"

"No. I haven't told anyone who isn't related to me by blood. Not even Mama Peaches." He shrugged, feeling a little guilty about that. "And right now, there's not much to tell. But I didn't come here to talk about me or about Cammie. I came to see how you were doing."

"Okay, sweetheart. I get it. And I'll leave the topic alone... after I say this. I think your Uncle Lou's idea is a good one. I know your pride is a little hurt over what happened at the town hall meeting. But I urge you to objectively reconsider his suggestion. It just might be the best decision you ever make."

Kai forced a smile and squeezed his mother's hand. The prospect of him salvaging his friendship with Cammie seemed to bring her so much joy. He couldn't bear the thought of letting her down. "I'll give it some thought, Ma. I promise."

She nodded her approval. Then asked tentatively, "Have

you run into Michael and Marianne since you returned to town?"

"No." Kai groaned quietly, shaking his head. "And I don't want to."

"Kai." His mother placed a gentle hand on his arm. A warning not to say or do anything he might regret. "Please don't—"

"No more talk about the Anthonys." His eyes met hers. "Please."

She nodded and touched his cheek. "C'mon out back. Let me show you where I'm planting the garden."

Kai followed his mother out to her raised garden beds in the backyard, thankful for the reprieve.

Now he only wished he could banish thoughts of Cam from his head so easily.

CAMILLA

*C*amilla cut her father a generous slice of her homemade rum cake, made from his mother's recipe. It was his very favorite dessert. Then she cut a piece for her mother who assessed her suspiciously.

"Camilla Denise Anthony..." Her mother accepted the plate and fork, setting both on the table. She leaned back in her seat, with her arms folded. "What is going on?"

"What do you mean?" Cam cut another slice of cake for herself, not meeting her mother's gaze.

"I mean, there's something you want to tell us, but you feel the need to put us in a food coma first." Her mother narrowed her gaze.

"Marianne, you're overthinking this. Can't you just relax and let me enjoy my favorite dessert?" her father grumbled as he put another slice of the moist, delicious cake in his mouth.

"Tell me I'm wrong." Her mother stared across the table at her.

"Fine." Cam sighed. "But it's not a big deal or anything."

"But it is *something*." Her father raised a brow, but he didn't allow it to interfere with him eating his rum cake.

Cam cleared her throat and sat up straight. "There's a project Uncle Lou is offloading that I'd like to take on."

"You've done that lots of times before." Her father shrugged in between bites of his cake. "Why is this project different?"

"Because it would be bigger than any project I've ever taken on before. It's not a single home or apartment building. It's an entire neighborhood and a school, which we'll convert into apartments."

"That's a pretty big project, Cam. Think you're ready to take that on?" Her father met her gaze as he took another bite of cake.

"I'm definitely ready for this project," she said assuredly as she poked her slice of cake with her fork.

"What does Uncle Lou think about Charming Home Design taking on that many projects all at once?" Her mother asked.

Camilla sucked in a deep breath. Damn, her mother knew her well. And she knew Uncle Lou well, too.

"Uncle Lou has some concerns about whether my team can manage this entire project on our own."

"Or raise the cash for it, I'd assume." Michael Anthony pointed his fork in her direction.

"And that," Cammie conceded taking a bite of the moist, delicious cake.

"So exactly how much is this slice of cake gonna cost me?" Her father chuckled.

"Nothing, Dad. You're out of the business. I know that, and I'd never try to drag you back in. Nor would I ask you for money."

Her parents had a decent savings, but they weren't quite sixty. As far as she was concerned, they had plenty of life ahead of them. So they'd need that money if they were to continue living comfortably.

Her father looked relieved, but her mother looked even more concerned. "If you're not looking for an investor, what is it that you're not telling us?" she asked.

Cam put down her fork. "Uncle Lou doesn't believe I'm ready to handle a project this big on my own. Kai Arrington wanted to purchase it, but Uncle Lou doesn't want to see this neighborhood gentrified. So he proposed that—"

"Lou wants the two of you to work together?" Her mother's eyes widened, as if the idea was horrific.

"Yes." Cam's tone was matter-of-fact as her gaze shifted from her mother's to her father's. "He vouches for Kai and for the quality of his work. Uncle Lou thinks that with the two of us working together, we'll balance each other out."

Her parents looked at each other, slight panic gripping both of them. Her father's fork hit his plate with a clang as he dropped it.

"Camilla, you know how Kai feels about our family and about your father." Her mother stood, pacing the floor. "I'm surprised he would agree to a collaboration."

"He hasn't," she admitted. "Not yet, anyway. And to be honest, I was completely against the idea at first, too. But Uncle Lou is right. Together, we could make this a truly amazing renovation project. Create beautiful, affordable homes that the community could be proud of."

"And you really think Kai will agree to that?" her father asked.

"Yes, I do. Eventually. He just needs a little more prodding."

"Camilla, I know you're still holding onto the image of that handsome boy you once adored." Her mother's tone and expression softened. "But do you really believe you can trust him, sweetheart? Kai has spent more than half of his life believing that your father betrayed his. That we're his enemies. Now he's suddenly going to suspend that belief to do this deal with you?" Marianne Anthony shook her head, her arms folded tightly, and her hands balled into fists. "I don't believe it, not even for an instant."

"The last time I saw Kai Arrington, he swore he'd get even with me for what I did to his father," her dad reminded her. "What if this whole collaboration thing is just an attempt to get back at me through you, Cam? Kai knows you've always had a soft spot for him."

Well, this isn't going the way I hoped.

Cam was a grown woman. She didn't need her parents' approval. But deep down, she couldn't help wanting it.

She wanted her father to be proud of her for taking this next step in her business. And she wanted her mother to be pleased that she'd taken the first step toward healing the rift between the Arrington and Anthony families.

"Back then, Kai was an angry, hurt, confused teenager who'd just lost everything, Dad. Did he do and say some incredibly dumb things? Absolutely. But do you really think he'd hurt me to get back at you?"

"We never really know what anyone is truly capable of, Camilla." There was a flash of warning in her mother's dark eyes. "None of us believed Barris was capable of embezzlement and money laundering until he actually did it."

A valid point.

Still, she didn't believe Kai was capable of that kind of treachery. He was a good guy, if naïve in his continuing belief that his father was falsely accused.

But didn't every child want to believe the best of their parents, regardless of their age?

"Look, I appreciate your concerns, and I value your opinions," Camilla said. "But this is something I need to do. So I'm not here to ask you for permission. I just wanted you to hear this from me." She stood and pushed her chair under the table and started collecting the dishes. "Kai may never go for this deal, but it won't be for lack of trying on my part."

Camilla gathered the dishes and took them to the kitchen, hoping that Kai truly was the good, kind, trustworthy person she'd always believed him to be.

CAMILLA

*I*t'd been nearly a week since Kai had kissed Camilla in the parking lot of the Renaissance Lounge. She'd waited a few days before calling him, just so he wouldn't get the wrong idea. But according to his assistant, he would be working out of his North Carolina office most of the week. She'd left messages for him in Pleasure Cove with no response.

Kai was dodging her. Lou wasn't willing to budge. Her parents still believed that working with Kai would be a terrible mistake. And she was fresh out of ideas.

Defeated, Camilla slipped into the chair in front of Uncle Lou's desk and groaned. "I've tried everything, Uncle Lou. Last week I thought I was this close to getting Kai onboard with the project." She peeked through her forefinger and thumb. "But I haven't been able to get a hold of him all week and he hasn't returned any of my calls."

Lou was bent over his desk with his reading glasses on, reviewing some paperwork. He didn't look up. "You've tried *everything*?"

"Yes. Everything. I appealed to reason. I pointed out how

profitable the project could be. I highlighted the fact that this was the perfect in for future building projects in Southlake Park. I even suggested that this project could be a tribute to his dad and the neighborhood should bear his family's name." Cammie rattled off each item, ticking them off on her fingers.

"Did you talk to Mama Peaches?" He kept scanning his document.

Cam shrugged, adjusting in her seat. "I was saving that as a last resort."

"I think you're there." He finally looked up, peeking at her over his reading glasses. "As much as I'd like to, I can't hold out on this project forever, Cam. The word has gotten out and other developers have shown interest. I can give you another two weeks before I start entertaining other offers. No more. So if you really want to make this work--"

"I get it, Uncle Lou." Camilla stood. "I guess I'm going to see Mama Peaches."

"Cam, I know you're hesitant because you believe Peaches has always taken the Anthonys' side in all this. Maybe you even think that she doesn't much like your family."

"Are you saying that isn't true?" Camilla folded her arms.

"I'm saying I've known Peaches Brighton for more than fifty years, and the woman has never ceased to amaze me. If you give her a chance, I think she might surprise you, too."

"I hope so, Uncle Lou. Because everything is riding on it."

Lou gave her a kind smile, then returned his attention to the papers sprawled on his desk. "I talked to Peaches right before you arrived. She and Deen were headed to Hammond Deli. Maybe you'll have better luck there this time."

Cam thanked Lou and hurried to her car, heading to Hammond Deli. Everything she knew about the woman who'd helped raise Kai and countless other young men in the neighborhood indicated that she would take Kai's side.

Maybe Mama Peaches would be as opposed to their collaboration as her parents were. But time was running out and she was flat out of options.

Mama Peaches was her only hope.

~

Cam approached the table where Mama Peaches sat embroiled in a heated discussion with her best friend, Ms. Geraldine.

"Hello, Mama Peaches, Ms. Geraldine." She cleared her throat, her heart racing as both women stopped arguing and turned their attention toward her. "I don't know if either of you remember me, but—"

"Child, don't be silly. Of course, we know who you are," Mama Peaches said. "You're Michael and Marianne Anthony's girl."

"Seen you on every one of those morning shows you did," Ms. Geraldine added. "And that time you were on that do-it-yourself network. They should give you one of those shows of your own. You're a pretty girl and you've got the personality for it."

"Thank you so much, Ms. Geraldine." Cam rubbed her hands on her jeans, her palms suddenly feeling sweaty. "Mama Peaches, do you think that we could talk for a few minutes...alone?"

"Now why is it that everyone seems to think I can't keep a secret?" Ms. Geraldine huffed, suddenly indignant.

"I didn't mean to imply--"

"Because you're like a busted refrigerator, Deen. You can't keep nothin'!" Mama Peaches said, as if it should be obvious.

"Now you know that ain't right, Peaches. I ain't told nobody about that boil you had to have removed from your--" The woman slapped a hand over her own mouth as her friend peered at her angrily. "Yeah, guess I see what you mean. But what am I supposed to do while you two have this private chit chat? I ain't finished my sandwich yet."

"How about you go and straighten out that crooked wig of yours?" Mama Peaches suggested matter-of-factly. "Might want to get all that spinach out ya teeth, too, while you're at it. Got enough spinach in them dentures to make a side salad."

Geraldine covered her mouth with one hand and grabbed her purse with the other before she stormed off to the restroom.

Mama Peaches chuckled as she watched her friend's retreating back. She turned to Cam. "You gon' stand there all day or we gon' have this conversation you want to have about Kai?"

Cammie slipped into the side of the booth that Ms. Geraldine had vacated. "How did you know--"

"What other reason would you need to have a private conversation with me?" Mama Peaches chuckled.

"Maybe I want to talk about the restoration of Southlake Park."

"You're an outspoken advocate of restoring Southlake Park, and I admire your passion for the neighborhood. But you've always worked directly with the Southlake Park Revitalization Association. Never sought out me and Deen before. And you wanted a private audience." Chuckling, Mama Peaches set her sandwich down and wiped her hands on a napkin. "Been alive twice as long as you, boo. Not much gets past me."

"Okay, you're right. I do want to talk about Kai. But I also want to talk about revitalizing the neighborhood." Cam gripped her hands beneath the table.

"I'm listening." The older woman pressed her back against the booth.

Camilla told Mama Peaches about the Marigold Circle cul-de-sac project Uncle Lou needed to offload and why he wasn't willing to let either her or Kai take on the project separately.

"So Lou suggested that the two of you work together on the project instead?" Mama Peaches chuckled a bit louder. "That Lou. Didn't think he had it in him."

"Ma'am?"

"Never mind." Mama Peaches waved a hand. "I think it's a brilliant idea. But let me guess, with a bit of reluctance, you signed onto the idea, but Kai don't want no parts of it. Not even after that kiss y'all had in the parking lot at Lou's boy's birthday party?"

"How did you--"

"Let's just say Deen ain't the only one around here that can't keep nothing." She laughed.

Cam's face was hot. She stammered. "That wasn't a real kiss. It was just meant for Derrick. I wanted him to think that Kai and I were together, so he'd stop trying to get with me."

"Well your plan worked. Now most of the neighborhood knows about that kiss and are speculating 'bout how long y'all have been together."

"We're obviously not together. If we were, I wouldn't be forced to come to you for help on this." Cam's voice trembled, but she was careful to keep her tone respectful. "Do I miss having Kai as a friend? Yes."

"But you do find him attractive.," It wasn't a question. "It was no secret back then how much you adored the boy. Looks like not much has changed."

Camilla's face was hot. She leaned back against the booth, her eyes not meeting Mama Peaches'. "With all due respect, Mama Peaches, I'm not asking for a matchmaker, here. I'm here because, like you, I adore Southlake Park. I love everything about this neighborhood. The people, the great old homes, the architectural styles, neighborhood fixtures like Hammond Deli with all of its history."

Camilla sighed. "This Marigold Circle project…it's just the kind of thing you and Ms. Geraldine and most of the folks at the revitalization association want. We can revive the neighborhood and convert the school to brand new, affordable housing. You know I'm a staunch opponent of gentrification. However, I do believe that there can be a place for some of these newer, high-end homes with a higher price point that will draw in new, high-income residents. This project is the perfect place to show how the two can be blended, and it can be done well."

Mama Peaches drew in a deep breath and sighed. "It all sounds good on paper, Camilla. But what about the reality of working every day with Kai when you two obviously have very different ideas about gentrification?"

"I'm no withering violet, Mama Peaches. I can handle it, and I can handle, Kai. And by the end of the project, I know he'll get it. Because he's a good guy, and he loves this neighborhood, too. I just need him to give this a chance. And I've exhausted every avenue I have to make that happen. So, I'm here, begging you for any advice, any insight you have to offer." She wiped away the dampness that momentarily clouded her vision.

Mama Peaches stared at her for a moment, her head tilting as she assessed her. She sighed quietly and nodded.

"Okay, Camilla, if you want to get Kai on board, here's what you need to do…"

MEKKAI

*K*ai stood backstage at the Southlake Park Cultural Center, where the Southlake Park Bachelor Auction was being held. He clutched a bouquet of white roses. Business and personal issues had kept him in Pleasure Cove longer than he'd expected. He'd skated back into town last night.

First thing Monday morning, he was headed right back to Pleasure Cove to finish up a crucial project because his foreman had suddenly taken ill. Kai trusted his crew, but this project was just too important to leave to chance. Hopefully, whoever won the bid tonight would understand.

The hosts of the evening's festivities, Mama Peaches' son Jeremy Brighton and Ms. Geraldine's granddaughter, Naima Grant, stepped out on the stage to much applause. Kai had peeked through the curtain earlier and it was standing room only out there. The auditorium was filled with women waving money who were ready to start the bidding.

Naima introduced the first of the bachelors up for auction, Jacob St. Williams, president of the Urban Choice

Channel. Then Jeremy, the bid catcher, started calling out the bids. The bachelor eventually went for one-thousand dollars.

The next bachelor, Phil Hart, now a doctor of endocrinology got the women in a furious bidding war. He finally went for $2500.

Impressive.

Kai's heart beat faster with every bachelor that went on stage before him. But now he was up, Bachelor #3.

It was a silly auction. He didn't lack self-confidence and had no doubt about his appeal or what he brought to the table. Yet, his heart raced, and his hands trembled slightly with each step he took toward that stage.

"And now we have another of Southlake Park's sons, Mekkai Arrington, The Perfectionist," Naima announced, her broad smile calming his nerves a bit. "He's good with his hands, aims to please, and won't stop until he gets it right." Naima fanned herself for effect and many of the ladies in the audience did, too. "Kai loves surfing and spends as much of his free time on the beach as possible. And he's the CEO of his own company, so he likes being large and in charge. This is gonna be a hot one, so get those paddles ready, ladies."

"All right now," Jeremy stepped forward. "Who is going to start the bidding at—"

"Five hundred," a familiar voice chirped. "I want to start the bidding at five hundred dollars."

Kai stared out at the crowd, beyond the blinding lights.

Camilla?

What on earth was she up to?

"Okay ladies, we have a generous opening bid," Jeremy said over the murmurs in the crowd. The enthusiastic women up front seemed personally offended by Cam's decision to flout the usual bidding routine by calling out her own bid. "Anyone want to give this lovely lady a little competition?" He glanced around the crowd. "Do I hear six hundred?"

"Six hundred." One of the ladies raised her paddle, clearly a little miffed.

"Six hundred!" Jeremy acknowledged the woman. "Do I hear--"

"One thousand dollars." Everyone's heads turned toward Camilla again.

The whispers in the crowd grew louder.

"Well damn. Can a bitch get a shot at bidding?" a woman upfront, wearing a tight, red dress and silver shoes two sizes too small grumbled.

"I've got one thousand dollars. Eleven-hundred anyone?"

"Twelve-hundred!" And older woman shouted, raising her white paddle. She whispered loudly to her friend, "She ain't the only one who can skip a couple hundreds."

"Fifteen hundred." Camilla was unfazed by the woman's bid.

"Sixteen hundred?" Jeremy scanned the crowd.

The older woman raised her paddle and opened her mouth to bid.

Camilla suddenly shot to her feet, her paddle raised and fire raging in her eyes. "Twenty-one hundred dollars."

The crowd roared and most of them looked from Camilla to the older woman she'd gotten into a bidding war with.

"Twenty-two hundred dollars anyone?" Jeremy scanned the crowd. The older woman declined, and no one else uttered a word. "Twenty-one hundred going once...going twice...Sold!" He slammed the gavel against the sound block, then pointed it at Camilla. "To the lovely lady in the black dress."

Kai was still stunned, adrenaline pumping through his veins as he exited the stage, making way for the next bachelor. At a little area on the side of the room, a photo was taken as he handed the bouquet of white roses to Camilla.

Her curls were pulled to one side, falling over her shoulder. The short, black wrap dress she wore clung to her delicious curves for dear life. Her subtle makeup left her skin looking soft and natural. And the cherry red lipstick she wore drew his attention to her mouth, igniting memories of the intense kiss they shared.

"Thank you for not letting me languish up there," Kai said as they walked toward the back of the room. The bidding went on furiously behind them. "Or worse, I could've gone to someone who'd be wrapped around me like an octopus right now."

"How do you know that what I have in mind for you isn't worse?" She folded her arms. An innocent act which pushed her breasts higher, revealing more of her warm brown skin above the low-cut neckline of her black dress.

"True." He swallowed hard, raising his eyes to meet hers. Neither of them spoke for a moment. Then he asked, "Why did you do it?"

"Why'd I bid for my rival on the Marigold Circle deal?" Cam clutched her black and silver beaded bag in her hand as she studied his face. "Because I want a fair shot."

"At?"

"At proving what an asset I can be to you on this project. And at making you see that you can make a real, life-changing difference for families here in Southlake Park if you're willing to make just a few adjustments."

Kai groaned. They were back to talking about the deal. "Look, I promised to consider it and I did, but—"

"Then let me show you what I can do. Give me a chance to prove that we can work well together." She placed a hand on his arm.

Kai glanced down at her hand. He could feel the heat of

her skin through the fabric of his gray suit. His eyes met hers. "You sure that's the only reason you bid for me like that?"

His voice was teasing, but the question was a serious one. He'd been thinking of her and of their kiss since Landis's birthday party. A part of him wondered if she felt the same.

"Get over yourself, playboy." She playfully punched his gut.

He didn't flinch.

Cam's gaze turned heated when her hand hit the solid wall of muscle. She cleared her throat. "This is a business deal. Pure and simple."

"Good." He couldn't tear his gaze away from her full, lower lip. "As long as we're both clear on that."

"Crystal. Now, about this date I just laid down twenty-one hundred dollars for..." Her defiant gaze had returned along with a wide grin. "I hear you need help on a really important project, and I've always wanted to visit North Carolina."

Mama Peaches.

He glanced around the room looking for the only person who could've told Cam about his dilemma back in Pleasure Cove. When he returned his gaze to Cam, she could barely contain her grin.

"What about your business here?"

"Things are slow right now. Besides, I trust my crew implicitly, and we're at a point where I feel confident handing the project off for a week." Her smile deepened. "Any more objections?"

"If you do this, I'm going to put you to work. It won't be glamorous. I need help with painting and bathroom tile."

"I might primarily do design now, but I cut my teeth in this business doing paint and tile on one of Uncle Lou's crews. And I do a little of each on nearly every reno I do, just to keep my skills sharp." She leaned in and straightened his pocket square. "We can iron out the details over brunch tomorrow at Miss Maybelline's at say…eleven? My treat."

"Noon, and I'm treating." It was no use arguing with Camilla, and he could honestly use her help. But he wouldn't let her get away with thinking she was calling all the shots.

CAMILLA

amilla stepped out of the ride share and surveyed the cheerful, three-story beach house with periwinkle clapboard and fresh, white trim situated steps away from the Atlantic Ocean.

Pleasure Cove was gorgeous.

No wonder Kai maintained a residence here, even after his return to Chicago. Thankfully, the house he owned was a large rental home with five bedrooms, four of which afforded an incredible ocean view. he'd suggested she stay in one of his guest rooms.

If he wasn't for the fact that he'd promised to put her to work, it would practically be a vacation. Still, according to the rental home website, there was a private, heated pool and a fire pit. So she was determined to get in a little downtime, even if it was after they'd come crawling home at midnight.

"Sorry I couldn't pick you up at the airport this afternoon." Kai appeared suddenly and made his way down the incredibly long flight of stairs leading to the front porch on the second floor. "But I had an important appointment that I couldn't miss."

His gaze shifted from hers to the ride share driver's as he took her luggage from the older man.

"I realize this isn't a social visit. You don't have to get my luggage. I can handle it." She reached for her bags, but he didn't move.

"Or you can just allow me to be the gentleman that my mother and Mama Peaches raised me to be." He cocked his head, studying her. "If that's not too much trouble."

"No." She extended her hand, indicating that she would follow him. "By the way, the pictures on the website don't do the place justice. It's even more impressive in person. Did you update the beach house yourself?"

"I did. Thank you." He seemed surprised by her genuine compliment.

"Was this your first rental space?" She followed him through a door on the lower floor.

"Yes." He opened a door, revealing an indoor elevator. "But my first solo renovation project was my mom's cottage up the beach."

Ms. Lana.

His mother had always been gorgeous. There was something truly regal about her. And she'd always been sweet and kind. Generous. Kai had been so much like her in those ways. But when his father had been convicted and sent to prison and his mother had fallen ill, so many of those traits that reminded Cammie of his mother seemed to have died. Or at the very least, they'd gone into hiding, leaving behind an angry teenager who blamed the world.

"How is your mother?" Cam asked as Kai pushed the elevator button and the car began its ascent to the top floor.

"My mother is good." He said quietly. "But you can see that for yourself."

The doors slid open and Ms. Lana stood there, one trem-

REESE RYAN

bling hand pressed to her lips and her dark eyes filled with tears.

"Camilla." The older woman took tentative steps forward as she opened her arms to her. "It's so good to see you, sweetie."

"Auntie Lana." Cam's eyes burned with tears and fat drops spilled onto her cheeks as she rushed into the woman's open arms. "It's good to see you, too."

There were so many words she wanted to say. So many apologies she wanted to make. But their hug, which seemed to go on forever and yet, not nearly long enough, conveyed all of the things that she couldn't.

"Okay, you two. Enough of the blubbering," Kai teased, approaching from the opposite direction. He'd obviously taken her bag to her room and returned without either of them noticing. Kai extended a box of tissue to them. "You're happy to see her, she's happy to see you, and the world is a beautiful place."

"It is indeed." Lana's soft smile warmed her chest. She pressed a hand to Camilla's cheek. "You were an adorable little girl, but you've become such a gorgeous, impressive woman." Lana's smile turned sad. She dropped her hand from Cam's cheek and wrapped an arm around her waist. "Your parents must be so proud of you." She whispered the words softly in her ear as they trailed Kai down the hall. "How are Michael and Marianne?"

"They're good." Sadness filled Camilla's chest, too. The pain and distance of the past twenty-five years slowing filling the space that had been overcome with joy and love at seeing the woman she once adored so. "And they send their love."

Lana seemed relieved. She tightened her grip on Cam's waist and nodded. "Be sure to send mine back to them, too."

"I hope this will do," Kai's curt tone indicated that he'd

overheard their conversation. And that he didn't appreciate his mother's glowing mention of her parents.

Camilla glanced around the room. A king-size bed. Walls painted seafoam green. The bedding, pillows, and accessories in coral, teal, turquoise, and light gray balanced the color on the walls quite nicely. A door led to a balcony that ran the length of the house and large windows overlooking the Atlantic Ocean spilled light into the room.

"It's perfect," she said, staring out onto the sea for a moment before turning back to Kai and his mother. "I'll be very happy here. Thank you."

Lana's smile deepened, but Kai's expression was unreadable.

"Well, we'll let you settle in. Come down whenever you're ready. I've prepared a late lunch," his mother said.

"That sounds wonderful." She was starving. Didn't anyone serve real food on flights anymore? "Then we'll head over to the project site?"

"There'll be plenty of time for that." Kai shoved his hands in his pockets. "And there's lots to do. So just eat and relax today. Maybe go for a swim. The pool is heated and there's a hot tub out there."

"Everything you need is laid out in the bathroom, sweetheart." Lana grinned, slipping her arm through Kai's. "We'll see you when you come downstairs. There's no rush."

After the door clicked, Camilla turned back to study the view. The pool was just beneath her and the ocean was just beyond the dunes. A boardwalk led from the backyard to the beach.

This was a business trip and her goal was to convince Kai that they should team up on the Marigold Circle project. She wouldn't lose sight of that. But that didn't mean she couldn't spend a little time enjoying herself, too.

MEKKAI

*E*vening was falling and the temperature had begun to drop. Still, it was far warmer than the high temperature back in Chicago. Kai glanced through the kitchen window as he prepared the fire pit outside. His mother threw her head back and laughed at something Cammie said. She looked genuinely happy. Happier than he'd seen her in some time.

After all these years, he still found himself monitoring his mother's state-of-mind and emotions. Looking for any sign that she was about to fall off the cliff into the same abyss of despair that had nearly taken her from them all those years ago. When she, for a brief moment, believed that ending it all with a bottle of pills would be less painful than the notoriety of living as the wife of a disgraced, imprisoned, and murdered man.

Kai had been the one to discover her laying on the floor of her bedroom in their family home, soon to be repossessed by the bank. He'd been the one who'd worked so hard to keep the truth from everyone but Mama Peaches. He hadn't even told his younger brother the truth. Instead he'd told him that Ma was sick. The same thing he'd said to everyone.

Still, in a tight-knit community like Southlake Park, it wasn't long before the truth got out. He could still remember the pain on his little brother's bloodied, bruised face when he returned to Mama Peaches' house, clothes ripped and his lip cut and bleeding.

Keith had learned the truth from cruel children teasing him about a mother who'd rather be gone than to raise her own children.

Even back then, he realized that the situation was far more complicated than that. He never doubted for a minute that his mother loved them. But much like him, she'd been unable to see past her own despair and pain.

It'd been years before he'd seen his mother smile again. And the rift between Keith and his mother had taken more than a decade to heal. His mother was good now, and he wouldn't allow anyone to jeopardize that. But she'd insisted that she wanted to see Camilla. That it would be good for her.

From the laughter between them, it seemed his mother was right. He'd been trying to protect her from the past, but perhaps this was all a part of the healing process.

For his mother and for him.

Camilla Anthony had insinuated herself into his life and he'd been forced to confront his painful past. The knot of anger and resentment lodged in his chest was slowly unfurling. It felt as if he could breathe more easily, a sense of lightness left in its place.

"Is the fire ready, son?" His mother stood on the balcony just outside the kitchen, a heavy blanket draped over her arm.

"It is." He held his hands to the flame.

His gaze shifted to Camilla, who'd just stepped out of the

sliding glass door. She wore a casual, long-sleeve dress that grazed her toned thighs, revealing miles of smooth brown skin.

The wide grin on Cammie's face as she stepped outside and took in the ocean view, was contagious. Inside, he couldn't help smiling, too.

"Got all the makings of s'mores." Camilla held up a basket triumphantly as she descended the stairs.

"Cammie has never had s'mores. Can you believe that?" His mother sat in her favorite chair beside the fire. "It's a travesty, really. One we must rectify as soon as possible."

His mother reached inside the basket and threaded marshmallows on three extendable skewers they used for the fire pit. Each had a different color at its base. She handed one to each of them and kept the final one for herself.

They roasted marshmallows and he couldn't help being amused by Cam assembling her s'more and taking her first bite of the marshmallow, graham cracker, and chocolate creation.

"My God, that's good," Cam exclaimed around a mouthful of the sweet, sticky treat. "Where have you been all my life?"

"It's not like you haven't been to the beach before." Kai chuckled.

"But we never stayed after dark when we went to Greywood Beach," she said of the local beach their families had often gone to together when they were kids. "And we definitely didn't make s'mores. I would've remembered this gooey, sweet, crunchy goodness." She licked her fingers.

His heart skipped a beat. The innocent action was burned on his brain. Erotic thoughts of him and Camilla were as vivid as the sun setting in the sky overhead. He shifted in his seat to mask his body's reaction.

"Son, did you hear me?" Both his mother and Camilla

were staring at him. There was a mischievous glint in Cam's eye. As if she could see exactly what he'd been thinking.

"No, I didn't hear you, Ma. Sorry. I was just going over the plans for the project tomorrow in my head." He took a bite of his s'more.

"Oh great, I'd love to hear the plans," Cam said eagerly.

"And that's my cue to leave." His mother leaned over to kiss him on the cheek. Then she kissed Camilla's cheek and hugged her. "Good night, sweetie. This is my workaholic child. Don't let him work you too hard. I know this is a trip, but I hope you get to have some fun, too. I'd love to take you into town for lunch one day, if you have the time."

"I'd love that. Thank you, Auntie Lana. Good night."

"I'll walk you out." He followed his mother toward the door that led inside and through the first floor.

"Do you mind if I take a quick swim?" Camilla called.

The thought of Cam in a swimming suit did things to him. "Help yourself," he said without turning around or breaking his stride.

soon as he stepped inside. "Oh honey, Cammie is absolutely gorgeous. She's such a bright, wonderful, sweet girl. I hate that I missed so much of her life. And I've missed her mother. Marianne was my best friend, and I turned my back on her family."

"You turned your back on *them?*" Kai was indignant that his mother would make such a statement. "You didn't do anything wrong, Ma. It was Michael Anthony who—"

"Did what he had to do to protect himself and his family." His mother's voice trembled, and her dark eyes were shiny with tears. "He did what he had to do," she repeated quietly. "Even though it broke his heart."

Kai's spine stiffened. He jerked his arm from his mother's grasp. He couldn't believe what she was saying.

"Is that what Cam told you?" he demanded.

Had that been Camilla's endgame all along? To force her way into their lives and fuck with their heads? If so, he'd send her packing right now. Because he wouldn't allow anyone to jeopardize his mother's mental and emotional health.

"One day with Cam and suddenly you're siding with her father over Dad?"

"I'm not siding with anyone, honey. I'm just…" She sighed and pressed her back against the wall. His mother raised her eyes to his again. "I'm finally strong enough to tell you the truth. Your father did the things he was accused and convicted of. I begged him to tell you and your brother the truth, rather than allowing you to blame Michael, who was as much a victim in all this as we were. Barris kept promising he'd tell you, but he could never bring himself to do it."

"No." Kai shook his head, his heart thumping in his chest. Suddenly, it felt difficult to breathe. He dragged a hand through his hair. "It's not true. It can't be true. I asked Dad flat out, and he swore to me that—"

"I know, baby." Tears streamed down his mother's face. "He couldn't bear the thought of you finally realizing that he wasn't the man you thought he was. We were all he had left, Kai. He didn't want to risk losing your love and respect. It meant more to him than anything in the world."

Kai studied her face. There was so much pain and anguish there. But there was also a sense of relief. As if a load of bricks had been lifted from her chest.

Something inside of him crumbled. As much as he didn't want to believe it, there was no doubt that his mother was telling the truth.

Everything he'd believed about his father was a lie.

His chest burned with anger, hurt, and embarrassment.

"I used to think folks in the neighborhood pitied me because my father had died. But that wasn't it at all, was it?

They felt sorry for me because I was stupid enough to truly believe he was innocent."

"You weren't stupid, Kai. He was your father. Your hero. The man you wanted to emulate. But despite all his bravado, I guess he needed your faith in him as much as you did." She wiped at the tears running down her face.

Kai pressed a hand to his mouth. Afraid of the things he might say to his mother. His heart beat a mile a minute, and his mind was spinning as he tried to process her words.

His breathing became more rapid and the anger and resentment he'd lived with for so much of his life built in his chest again. Only this time it wasn't directed toward Michael Anthony.

He was furious with his father for what he'd done to their family. And for what he'd done to the Anthonys. He was angry with his mother for keeping the truth from him. And he was disgusted with himself for allowing his admiration for his father to blind him to the truth.

He'd always thought of his father as charming and charismatic. But in all honesty, the man had simply been a world-class bullshitter. He'd conned Kai the same way he'd conned vendors, customers, and sometimes his mother.

"My entire life is based on a lie." His body vibrated with the anger raging in his chest, which he struggled to control. "Why didn't you tell me the truth?"

"I wanted to." She wrapped her arms around herself. "But that belief you had in your father…it was all you had left of him. I couldn't bear to take that away."

"Ma, as terrible as that would've been, the alternative was so much worse. I blamed an innocent man for our lives falling apart. And I turned my back on my friend out of some twisted sense of obligation to Dad when he was the one who was wrong." He glared at his mother, his jaw tense and his hands balled into fists at his sides.

"I'm so sorry, honey," she whispered, one hand pressed to her stomach. "I wanted to tell you so many times." She wiped away more tears. "But I'm as much of a coward as your dad was. I thought if I moved you away from Chicago, it would all fade away and both our families would heal. But talking with Cammie tonight...I realized that hasn't happened for any of us."

Lana walked over to him and pressed a gentle hand on his arm. He didn't pull away, but he couldn't bring himself to embrace her either.

Not yet.

"Cammie and I talked about a little of everything. We laughed and we cried. But the thing I realized tonight more than anything is that when I look in this sweet, amazing woman's eyes, the love and admiration she has for you is there, clear as day."

"You're being melodramatic, Ma."

"No, baby. I'm not." She pressed a hand to his cheek. "Camilla has been in love with you since she was about five years old, Kai. And I still see it now. I knew in that moment, I couldn't allow this to continue."

"So what did you think, Ma? You'd tell me, it'd wipe out a lifetime of pain for both of us, and we'd just...what? Get married or something?"

"Sounds naïve, I guess." She shrugged. "But yes, some version of that. Not because it's what I want for you, but because it's what you want for yourself."

"I don't—"

"Don't bother denying it, son. I see the love you still have for her, too. It's a different kind of love." One corner of her mouth curled in a smirk. "But I believe it's rooted in the deep affection you had for her then." She smiled faintly, a faraway look in her eyes. "You were her protector. You wouldn't let anyone lay a hand on her. And you endured her myriad of questions about everything."

"Not much has changed in that regard." He'd gotten so angry when Derrick brought Cammie up at the barbershop that day. It'd been such a visceral reaction. He clenched his fists, still regretting not punching the guy. "I'm not looking for a relationship, Ma. My life is in limbo right now. And until I know what my future looks like—"

"Talk to Camilla. Tell her everything. Maybe she—"

"I won't put that kind of burden on her," he countered quickly, tabling any further discussion of him and Camilla being anything more than friends. "I'm glad you finally told me the truth about Dad, but this doesn't change my situation when it comes to Camilla." He wished he could go back six months earlier and make a different choice. But actions had consequences. And he would own up to his.

"Maybe you're right, Kai. But Camilla Anthony is no damsel in distress. She's a strong, smart, capable woman. Tell her and let her make her choice."

"I can't talk about any of this right now." He ran a hand over his head and heaved a sigh. "Goodnight, Ma."

He turned and headed back through the door. He walked past Camilla doing laps in the pool, across the boardwalk suspended over the dunes, and onto Pleasure Cove Beach— the one place he'd always felt calm and where everything always made sense.

CAMILLA

*C*amilla stripped off her little dress, revealing the black bikini she'd worn underneath it. Then she grabbed a pair of goggles and dipped a toe into the pool. The heated water was warm and soothing. A contrast to the rapidly cooling air around her. She jumped into the small pool, completely immersing herself rather than submerging herself a little at a time.

That was the Camilla Anthony method.

Jumping in with both feet before she could talk herself out of something she wanted. Like Uncle Lou's proposed collaboration. Or falling for Mekkai Arrington.

Cam drew in a deep breath, then submerged her face in the water to begin swimming freestyle laps. She didn't get a chance to swim nearly as much as she'd like, but she loved the water.

On one of her final laps, she saw Kai storm back outside, past the pool and over the boardwalk toward the beach.

Something is wrong.

Was he upset about something she'd said to his mother?

Cam climbed out of the pool, water dripping from her

body and her hair. She wrapped herself in a towel, slipped into her flip-flops and followed Kai over the boardwalk to the beach.

Kai was sitting on the beach not far from where the waves crashed against the shore. He stared out onto the water, his arms folded over his knees.

There was overwhelming sadness in his expression as she settled onto the sand beside him. He didn't seem surprised that she was there.

Camilla stared out onto the moonlit water.

There was so much pain in his eyes.

"Did my visit upset your mother?"

"No." He shook his head, still staring ahead. "You coming here was a good thing."

Cam tugged on her earlobe to remove the water from her ear because surely, she heard him wrong. "I'm sorry, did you just say that you're glad I'm here?"

"Yes, Cam. That's exactly what I said." He turned to face her. "You're shivering." His eyes widened with alarm.

It wasn't until then that she realized her teeth were chattering. The night air had cooled considerably. "I'm fine, but something is obviously wrong with you."

He stood, dusting the sand off his bottom. "Let's get you into the hot tub and warm you up."

Kai reached down and pulled her up. She stood toe-to-toe with him, shivering. Her hair and body were dripping.

He wrapped the towel tightly around her.

"Hop in the hot tub, for a few minutes, at least."

"Alone? While you're fully dressed?" She met his gaze. "That'd be weird."

Without hesitation, he lifted the hem of his shirt and yanked it over his head, tossing it on the lounger. Then he shucked his jeans, revealing a pair of black boxer briefs. "Better?"

Much better.

"Sure." She shrugged as if it were no big deal. But her eyes traced the outline of his shaft beneath the fabric.

Kai removed the hot tub cover, turned it on, and hopped inside. Then he helped her in, too.

Cam sat on the bench, leaving a foot of space between them. She sank into the water, her eyes drifting closed as she allowed the warm bubbles to release the tension from her neck and shoulders. When she opened her eyes, Kai was staring at her.

"What is it, Kai?"

He shook his head, still staring at her as if she were a particularly challenging puzzle that needed to be solved.

"Will you at least tell me why you're suddenly glad that I came to visit?"

He frowned. His brows furrowed and there was a pained look on his face. He reached for her hand beneath the water. "I owe you a huge apology, Cam. You were right, and I was wrong."

"About collaborating on the project?" Her heart raced and she could barely conceal her excitement.

"No, about my father being a selfish prick who was guilty of everything he was accused of and more. And about your father not having a choice but to do what he did." He seethed, his jaw tense and anger flashing in his dark eyes.

Everything went still for a moment. She couldn't believe what she'd heard. "What changed your..." Cam pressed a hand to her mouth. "Aunt Lana. That's why you were gone so long. She told you the truth, didn't she?"

"I believed him all this time. I took that lying bastard at his word. He swore to me that--" Kai heaved a deep sigh and shook his head. "And I believed him. I was ready to burn down the entire fucking world to get justice for him, and he would've let me. I should've seen my father for what he was. If not back then, I should've at least seen it now."

The tortured look on Kai's face broke Cam's heart. How could Barris have done this to his son? To all of them?

"Of course, you wanted to believe in your dad, Kai." She slipped her hand into his beneath the bubbling water. "There's no crime in that. He was your hero. Some part of you *needed* to believe him."

"That doesn't excuse what I did. I'm sorry for being such an asshole to you, Cam. For disrespecting your father. For—"

"Throwing that brick through our living room window?"

"You knew that was me?" He grimaced as if the revelation had caused him physical pain.

"I was home sick from church that day. I heard the crashing glass and ran to my bedroom window. That's when I saw you running down the street in that yellow FUBU jacket you practically lived in back then," she said quietly.

She'd never admitted that to anyone. She'd held onto that ugly truth to protect her parents' feelings as much as she'd done it to protect Kai.

"But that was *after* I'd been so awful to you." He dragged a hand through his hair. "Why didn't you tell your parents? It would've been the perfect opportunity to get back at me."

Cammie shrugged, her gaze on their clasped hands beneath the water. "You were still my friend. You'd just lost your father. You'd almost lost your mother. You were out of your mind with grief. I didn't want to make the situation worse for you."

"I'd never have done that if I'd known you were there. I should never have done it at all. I don't expect your parents to forgive me. And I have no right to ask you to for—"

"I forgive you, Kai." Cam slipped out of his grip and placed her hands on either side of his face. Eyes drifting closed, she pressed her lips to his in a tentative kiss.

He was still for a moment. Not reciprocating, but not protesting. But then he wrapped his arms around her, pulling her body as tightly against his as their positions allowed. And his lips glided against hers in a kiss that was increasingly intense.

Suddenly, he broke their kiss. There was an apology in his expression as his eyes met hers. "Cam, I'm obviously attracted to you. And I want this...I want you. More than you know. But nothing that's happened tonight changes the fact that I'm not in a place in my life right now where getting into a relationship makes sense."

Cam forced a smile, her fingers trailing the hair on his chest. "I've done relationships and marriage. I'm not looking for forever, I'm just looking for right now. And right now, Kai, I want you."

Even as Cam said the words, she wanted to believe them. And if Kai had been any other man, what she said would've been true.

But Mekkai Arrington isn't just any other man.

Kai was her lifelong crush. The man she'd always wanted. The man she hadn't been able to stop thinking about for the past twenty-five years. Even if all she could do was resent him.

It was true, she hadn't been looking for forever. Her focus was on building her career and improving the community of Southlake Park. But then Kai came along, and everything changed.

Her priorities hadn't changed. She still wanted those things, but she wanted Kai in her life, too.

If all they'd ever have was tonight, that would have to be enough. At least she'd be able to get Kai Arrington out of her system and finally move on.

Kai assessed her as if deciding whether to buy the bullshit

she was trying to convince him and herself of. Maybe he needed to believe it as much as she did.

He kissed her and pulled her onto his lap, swallowing her soft groan as his steely length pressed against the sensitive space between her thighs. Her nipples beaded against his chest and her knees dug into the side of the hot tub as she ground her hips against him, wanting more of the delicious sensation.

He tore his mouth from hers and trailed kisses down her neck and shoulder, the warm bubbles still tickling her skin. Then he unfastened her bikini top, sliding it down one shoulder, then the other.

"Fuck," he whispered against her skin, trailing kisses lower until he closed his mouth over the beaded tip.

Cam gasped at the sensation of his warm mouth on her cool skin, pressing forward to give him better access. Camilla slid her fingers into the soft curls at his crown. She tipped her head back, soft moans escaping her mouth as she gave into the incredible feeling of being in Kai Arrington's arms.

Camilla had held so much anger toward Kai when she'd heard he'd returned to Chicago. She'd nursed the hurt he'd caused her for years. It'd been easier to think of him strictly as her rival. He and his company were the devil and they needed to be stopped. Despite all of that, the moment she'd laid eyes on him at that town meeting...*this* was the very moment she'd envisioned.

A small part of Camilla had dared to hope that she and Kai could one day become friends again. A deeper part of her, one she'd been afraid to acknowledge, wanted this.

Kai pressed his mouth to hers again in a greedy, delicious kiss that sent a ripple of need throughout her body. He gripped her hips, gliding her sex against his, escalating the sensation of intense pleasure slowly rolling up her spine.

Until her body shuddered, and her walls clenched as she whispered his name.

"If it didn't feel so damn good, I'd be embarrassed that you were able to get me there so easily. My bikini bottom didn't even come off." She caught her breath as Kai kissed her neck and shoulder.

He chuckled. "Don't worry, I plan to have you in my bed, ass up, and completely naked before this night is over," he promised, his lips pressed to her ear.

"Sounds like a plan I can get behind." She pressed a kiss to his mouth and stood. "Just lead the way."

MEKKAI

*K*ai pushed Camilla against the cold, hard shower tiles as he kissed her again. They'd showered, soaping up every inch of each other's bodies. And now all he wanted to do was worship that incredible body. The one he'd been admiring since he'd seen her in that little blue dress at the town hall meeting.

He gently placed his large hands around her throat as he tipped her chin and kissed her, his tongue gliding against hers. Camilla glided one hand over his ass, gripping the muscles there. Her other hand drifted between his thighs, fisting the base of his erection.

An involuntary groan escaped his mouth as she glided her fist up and down his painfully hard dick. He wanted to be buried, balls deep, in this incredible woman he was so damn proud of. The woman who'd always had his back, even when he didn't deserve it.

He wanted her more than anything.

The sensation was quickly building. His knees felt like they were buckling. He needed to shift the attention back to her. Put all of the focus on bringing her pleasure again.

He gripped her wrist so that she released him. Then he slowly sank to his knees and pressed her thighs open. Camilla braced her back against the wall, her heels lifting as she pushed against the floor with her toes.

Kai pressed his mouth to the space between her thighs. His tongue teased her slit.

"Oh my God, Kai." She gasped, shoving her fingers into his hair. "That feels *so* good."

He parted her gently with his thumbs, as he glided his tongue against her swollen clit. He relished the unique salty sweetness of the woman who'd driven him crazy and yet made him adore her for as long as he'd known her.

Kai pressed a finger inside her, then another as his tongue continued to move against the needy bundle of nerves. The movement of both his fingers and tongue increased as she stood higher on her toes, straining toward his mouth. Her murmurs grew louder, laced with praise, a string of curses, and unintelligible words that even she probably didn't understand.

He curled his fingers forward, gliding them in and out of her wet heat. Then he sucked on her distended clit until she'd practically screamed his name, her walls clenching around his fingers and her body shuddering.

Kai stood, kissing her neck as she panted, her heart racing. Then he dried her off and carried her to his bed. He sheathed himself, then slowly glided his painfully hard erection inside her, savoring every single sensation.

His body shuddered with pleasure, his sensitive flesh surrounded by her slick walls. He pressed his mouth to hers, their bodies moving together until they were both on the edge again.

"I told you I wanted you in my bed naked, ass up," he said with a rough growl as he pressed a kiss to her temple. He kneeled on the bed, gently slapping her thigh. "Now."

One side of her mouth curled in a sexy little smirk that made him want to devour her. She rolled onto her stomach and then got on all fours, teasing him by wiggling her perfect ass. Making him want to sink his teeth into her flesh.

Later.

For now, he'd just focus on bringing them both home.

He glided inside her, taking her from behind. He began with slow, easy movements. His speed and intensity increased, his pleasure spiraling with the escalation of her breathy moans.

When he moved one hand from her waist, slipping it into the wetness between her thighs.

"Oh God, yes. Yes!" Her body shuddered and clenched. Cam tumbled over the edge, taking him with her.

CAMILLA

*C*amilla awoke to the sound of a steady thumping. She rolled over in bed, but Kai was gone. She reached for her cell phone and checked the time. It was barely five in the morning.

Who in the hell is making all that noise?

They'd spent most of the night exploring each other's bodies and finding inventive ways to bring each other pleasure. Then they'd raided the refrigerator, famished. Between the two of them, they'd wiped out most of the leftovers from the wonderful meal Lana made. But they'd done very little talking about anything of real importance.

She was worried about Kai.

Though he'd tried to hide it, he was clearly shaken by learning the truth about his father. His world had just shifted in a way that she knew gutted him. He'd been desperate to feel anything other than the pain of his father's betrayal. And she was glad she could be there for him. Consoling the loss he felt so deeply through their physical connection.

Their night together was simply a distraction for him.

She realized that, not allowing herself to assign it any deeper meaning.

Cam slipped from beneath the cover wearing an over-sized black T-shirt that Kai had loaned her. She padded to the elevator in her bare feet and took it down to the first floor. She followed the sound, now louder, until she reached the workout room.

Kai wore basketball shorts slung low on his hips and a pair of boxing gloves as he whaled on a punching bag. Sweat dripped down his forehead and his back. There was so much power in each blow and so much pain and anger in his expression. His mouth was twisted. His eyes were laser-focused. He was so consumed with his effort; he didn't notice her standing there in the doorway.

"What did that punching bag ever do to you?" She tilted her head as she watched him.

"Camilla." Kai wrapped his arms around the swinging punching bag, stilling it. His chest heaved as he caught his breath. "I'm sorry, did I wake you?"

"You did." She yawned and ran a hand through her hair, frizzy and still damp from their shower. "But we have to be at the site early anyway. Maybe you can fill me in on the project over breakfast." She yawned again. "Pancakes and bacon okay?"

"Yeah, sure." He tugged off one glove, then pulled off the other before drying his face and chest with a towel and tossing it in a laundry bin. Something about him in that moment made him look more vulnerable than she'd ever seen him. Like a nerve was exposed that he couldn't bear for her to see. "Look, Cam...we really need to talk."

Camilla's heart thumped so hard that the sound filled her ears. Her pulse raced and a knot formed in her stomach.

She could do without Kai's it's-not-you-it's-me speech.

"No need. We both just got a little caught up in all the

emotions last night. You're not looking for anything serious, and neither am I." She forced a smile. "What happens at the beach, stays at the beach. We're good."

His expression didn't convey the relief she expected to see there. She'd just let him off the hook in the best way possible. Yet, he almost looked disappointed. Or maybe she was seeing exactly what she hoped to see.

If Kai wanted something more with her, he wouldn't keep reminding her that he wasn't looking for a relationship.

He stepped closer, lifting her chin so their eyes met. "Is that what you *really* want, Cam?"

"Yes, of course." She was a terrible liar. The words barely made it past her lips, and it hurt her to say them.

Kai dropped his hand from her chin, sliding both arms around her waist. His eyes didn't leave hers. "Does that mean you wouldn't be interested in showering together this morning?" His voice was gruff, his tone enticing.

Cam smiled, a genuine smile this time. She pressed her hands to his chest and leaned in. "I don't know. Are you planning to do that *thing* you did last time? Because seriously, who could say no to that?"

Kai laughed, his eyes dancing. His mouth curved in a mischievous smile. "I think that can be arranged, gorgeous."

"Good. But I thought we might start out with me returning the favor."

"Oh...shit. Yeah." He lifted her, throwing her over his shoulder. Kai turned out the lights and headed for the elevator with her laughing as she held onto his back, slick with sweat, for dear life.

So much for breakfast.

～

Camilla had worked with Kai's team on the renovation of a lovely little historic beach cottage for the past three days. She suggested updates for the kitchen's layout to improve its function, flow, and aesthetics while maintaining its charming original components. The fresh, white kitchen with its lower cabinets painted robin's egg blue would be perfect for renters who were nostalgic for the past, but also appreciated the convenience of the latest appliances.

She'd painted the kitchen and cabinets herself and helped Kai pick out tile for the cottage's two bathrooms. The original and the master suite bathroom Kai's team had created by adding onto the home.

They were able to locate reclaimed wood to give the floors in the addition a similar feel to the original part of the house. Once they were sanded and all of the floors were stained the same color, you'd hardly be able to tell where the old floors ended, and the new floors began.

Kai had dropped her off at his beach house early, then he'd gone to meet with a potential client.

Cam was sore, tired, and exhausted. But she wanted to make dinner tonight, rather than ordering out, as they typically did. Usually grabbing a bite to eat by the pool or in his bed after making love.

The past few days had been amazing. But their time together here was quickly coming to an end. The thought of going back to Southlake Park and pretending as if none of this ever happened between them made her heart ache. But that was exactly what she'd agreed to. Kai had never promised her anything more.

Camilla showered and changed. She was rummaging through Kai's large, double door, stainless steel fridge for the makings of dinner when the doorbell rang.

If she was lucky, maybe it was Aunt Lana popping in with something for dinner.

Cam approached the front door, but through one of the glass transoms on either side of the door, she could see the face of a woman she didn't recognize.

A solicitor maybe?

Camilla opened the door and smiled at the woman who was heavily pregnant. "Hello. Can I help you?"

"Not unless you can turn the clock back six months." The woman laughed bitterly. One hand was propped on her back. The other rested on her belly. She shifted slightly. "I'm sorry, I must've read the calendar wrong. I thought Kai's place wasn't being rented this week."

"I'm not a renter," Camilla said, a sense of dread growing in her belly. "Are you a friend of Kai's?"

"Not for a very long time." The woman laughed. "I'm his ex-wife, LaDonna. Everyone calls me LaLa."

"Oh." Cam nodded, leaning against the door. "Well, Kai isn't here, LaDonna. He probably won't be back for at least an hour. I'll tell him you came by."

"Look, no offense, hon, but I just climbed all the way up those stairs and I'm not ready to climb back down them. Besides, my car is in the shop, so I took a rideshare here. Is it okay if I wait for him inside? You won't even know I'm here. Promise." She raised her fingers in a scout's salute.

Camilla studied LaDonna. She was beautiful, with long, silky black hair that fell below her shoulders. Her brown skin glowed. She was at least a head taller than Camilla, even in the sparkly ballet flats she was wearing. She looked more glamorous in a tunic and leggings than Cam looked on her best day.

Everything about the woman screamed fashionista.

She could see why Kai would've been attracted to her.

Cam shrugged and stepped aside. "I guess Kai wouldn't mind. Come in."

"Thank you." LaDonna waddled inside. Even her waddle was sassy.

Figures.

"I'll just lie down on the sofa in the sitting room." The woman gestured to the space right off the kitchen. "I could use an hour nap. Creating and carrying around another human is exhausting. Don't let anyone tell you differently."

Cam forced a weak smile. A small part of her was envious of the woman. Maybe even regretted not trying to have children during her short marriage. Then at least there would've been something memorable and lasting about that period of her life. Instead, the five years she'd been married felt like a complete waste of both their time.

"Can I offer you something to drink? Or maybe a piece of fruit or a slice of pie?"

"Just water, but I'll grab one."

LaDonna slung the designer handbag hanging from her elbow onto the couch. She waddled to the mini refrigerator beneath the counter and pulled out a bottle of water.

"You were cooking dinner for two, I assume." LaDonna glanced at the chaos in the kitchen. "Sorry if I interrupted your groove." She cracked the seal on the bottle of water and cocked her head. "I was so busy telling you who I am that I didn't catch your name."

Because I didn't give it.

"I'm Camilla Anthony, an old friend of Kai's from Chicago. I'm helping out on the renovation of a little beach cottage." She leaned against the sink where she'd been scrubbing baby potatoes before the woman arrived. "I'm a designer and renovation specialist. I have my own company back in Chicago."

"Camilla Anthony," the woman repeated, tapping her chin

as if trying to remember something. Suddenly, her eyes widened. "Wait…you're *Cammie* Anthony? As in your fathers were once in business together?"

"Guilty." Camilla could only imagine the things Kai must've said about her and her family to his ex-wife.

"Does that mean he's given up his insistence that his dad is completely innocent?" LaDonna said incredulously, her words accompanied by a mocking laugh.

Camilla narrowed her gaze at the woman but didn't respond to her derisive comment. Instead, she turned her back to her and started scrubbing the small potatoes with a wire brush. "I'd better get back to dinner. Let me know if you need anything."

Cam snapped green beans, seasoned steaks, and prepared an apple crumb pie. She moved in silence while a thousand questions cycled through her brain.

If they were divorced, why was LaDonna here? And who was the father of her child?

As she cored, peeled, and sliced the apples, carefully arranging them in the pie crust she kept reminding herself that what she and Kai shared was only temporary. So it was none of her business.

But her heart hadn't gotten the memo.

MEKKAI

The clients had signed the deal and they were scheduled to break ground on their new build in a few months. It was something his sales manager could've easily handled. But he was in town and the couple were A-list clients, so he'd wanted to handle the deal himself.

After he'd picked up a couple of bottles of champagne to celebrate, Kai found himself hurrying home to Cammie. He missed having someone to come home to. Someone to share his bed every night, even if all they were doing was eating takeout and watching crime shows.

After spending the day onsite together negotiating changes to his plans or quibbling over paint colors, he still looked forward to their time together at the end of the day.

It was something he could easily become accustomed to.

Cam was an incredible woman. A savvy, talented creative professional who had no qualms about rolling up her sleeves and painting or installing a kitchen backsplash. She was willful and determined. Sweet and thoughtful, but also an unapologetic smart-ass. And she was funny as hell.

He adored her.

There was no denying it, though he'd certainly tried. His mother was right. His growing affection for the woman Camilla had become was rooted in the affection he'd held for her since they were kids. If he were being honest, he'd known from the moment he'd kissed Cam in that parking lot that he'd wanted something more with her.

Their first night together, he'd been overwhelmed with that same feeling. He wanted to tell Camilla everything, including the fact that he wanted more than just friendship. But she'd still been insistent that this was just a fling. So he'd held back the words he'd wanted to say and kept to their agreement.

But it wasn't sitting well with him. When he held her in his arms and stared into those lovely brown eyes, he was sure she felt more for him than she was letting on. Something he would get his shit together and talk to her about before they flew back to Chicago on Sunday evening.

He parked his truck outside and entered through the lower floor. Kai took the elevator to the second floor, his arms overladen with bottles of champagne, snacks for the Marvel movie they were going to watch later, a quart of strawberries, and a can of whipped cream.

Kai set the groceries on the counter and wrapped his arms around Camilla's waist. He kissed her neck, moving aside her hair, still damp from the shower. "Looks like you showered without me. Maybe I can tempt you with a bubble bath later."

Cam stiffened at his words rather than melting in his arms the way she normally did when he made such a suggestion.

"What's wrong, babe?" Kai frowned at the panic evident in her eyes when she turned in his arms.

She nodded her head toward the other room where his very pregnant ex-wife LaLa stood looking indignant with her arms folded over her burgeoning belly.

"LaLa, what are you doing here?" He made no move to remove his hands from Cammie's waist. He needed her to know they weren't doing anything wrong.

Still, she clearly felt uncomfortable. She took a step away from him, then turned back to the pie she was preparing. As if she were trying to make herself invisible without leaving the room.

"I came to bring you some good news since you haven't been answering my calls for the past few days. Though, now I can understand why you've been ignoring me and our son." She placed a hand on her belly.

"*Possible* son," he clarified. Though the damage had already been done.

Camilla dropped the knife, her finger dripping with blood.

"Let me get you a bandage." He reached for her hand, but she withdrew it.

"No, I'm fine." She rinsed her finger, then wrapped it with a paper towel. "I saw some bandages in the first aid kit in my bathroom. It seems you have enough on your plate." She bypassed the elevator and climbed the stairs to the top floor.

Kai groaned, rubbing a hand over his beard. He'd really fucked up this time. Compounded one problem with another.

And once again, his mother had been right. He should've told Camilla everything. Given her the choice to decide.

"Sorry to break up your little...whatever this is...but I thought you'd like to know what I learned from a friend." LaLa joined him in the kitchen.

"And what is that, LaLa?" He scrubbed a hand down his

face, not bothering to hide his exasperation with his ex-wife, the woman who may or may not be the mother of his child.

"There's a non-invasive paternity test they can do now, rather than waiting until the baby is born to confirm that you're the father." She folded her arms over her belly.

God, if he could rewind his life six months.

He wouldn't have drunk a bottle of Grey Goose on the anniversary of his father's death. And he damn sure wouldn't have opened the door when LaLa showed up on his doorstep.

Premium vodka and self-pity were precursors for extremely poor decision-making.

He leaned against the sink, his arms folded, and carefully considered the woman he'd once thought he wanted to spend forever with. LaLa was a lot like his father. A charming, polished, bullshitter. With LaLa, there was always more to the story. "But?"

"Why do you always have to be so cynical when it comes to me?" LaLa feigned insult, pressing a hand to her chest. When he didn't take the bait, she sighed and folded her arms, too. "The test is twenty-five hundred."

"For a pregnancy test?" Something didn't smell right. When it came to LaLa and his money, it never did.

"Don't be so cheap, Kai. It's not like you can't afford it." She studied her freshly-manicured nails.

Which meant the prenatal paternity test was probably fifteen-hundred and LaLa intended to pocket the additional grand. It was something she'd done throughout most of their marriage. Though it'd taken him a few years to realize it.

"We've waited this long." Kai shrugged. "What's a few more months? Besides, I'd prefer a more reliable DNA test once the baby is born." He opened one of the bags and set the groceries on the counter. "Anything else?"

"Fine." LaLa shrugged, trying her best not to show her disappointment. "If you're okay with waiting, so am I. I just thought you'd appreciate the chance to end the suspense so we can focus on more important things like decorating this little guy's room." She pressed a hand to her belly.

"As soon as we're done with the beach cottage and that new build, I'll send a couple of guys over to paint the baby's room. Just pick out the colors and design and text it to me." Kai's attention was drawn to the elevator. Cam had taken it from the third floor and then gone down to the ground floor.

She'd been calm when she was in the kitchen. But he could feel the quiet vibration of rising anger when he'd held her in his arms. And Kai couldn't miss the disappointment in Cam's eyes before she fled the kitchen with her finger bleeding.

"So it's that kind of party." LaLa indicated the bottles of champagne and the strawberries and whipped cream. "Are you celebrating the fact that you no longer hate Camilla Anthony and her family?"

His attention snapped to hers and he scowled. "Whatever is happening between me and Camilla is none of your business, LaLa. We might've gone half on a baby, but we are not in a relationship. Nor will we ever be again. I was clear about that from the beginning. Me and you…that can never happen again. *Ever*. We made each other miserable. I don't want that for either of us."

"Maybe it's all champagne, skinny dipping, and whipped cream in places whipped cream definitely shouldn't go. But just remember, Kai, our love was once all shiny and new, too." She smiled at him sweetly. "At least with me, you know exactly who you're getting."

"I do. And I don't want it." He put the strawberries and whipped cream in the fridge and closed the door. "Neither apparently did you. Or did you forget that you left me for someone else?"

It was a fact he was no longer bitter about. He and LaLa were better off apart. Still, it was the ace he played whenever necessary.

"You don't have to keep throwing it up in my face. It was a mistake. Humans make them, you know, Mr. Perfect." She pursed her lips and cocked a hip.

Kai laughed to himself. His ex's derisive nickname was the basis for the moniker he'd used in the Southlake Park Bachelor Auction. The very reason Cam was here with him now. The woman he was quickly falling for. The woman he wanted to get back to. She'd been patient long enough.

"Look LaLa, as you can see Cam has gone to a lot of effort to make dinner tonight. So if there's nothing else--"

"If you'd answered my calls, I wouldn't be here now." She snatched her designer bag off the couch and raked her fingers through her long, black hair. "And my car is in the shop. I took an Uber here. I was hoping you could give me a ride home."

He whipped out his phone and summoned a rideshare for her. "Done. Your ride will be here in ten minutes." He returned the phone to his back pocket. "I'll walk you out. And LaLa?"

"Yes?"

"Don't show up here again uninvited, unless it's an emergency. In which case, you should be calling nine-one-one first."

"I can see myself out," she sneered as she turned on her heels and headed for the front door.

Kai sighed, then stepped out onto the balcony overlooking the backyard. Cam was swimming freestyle laps in the pool, her arms slicing through the water with focus and precision.

She was definitely pissed.

It was time to tell Cam all of the things he'd wanted to say the morning she'd interrupted his workout. He just hoped it wasn't too late.

CAMILLA

*C*am lost count of how many laps she'd completed. It didn't matter how many she'd swam. It wasn't enough to make her forget the sight of LaDonna, glowing and pregnant, carrying Kai's child. Nor could it erase the smirk on the woman's face when she'd declared that she was carrying *their* son.

"Camilla, can we talk?"

She stopped mid-stroke and looked up at him standing by the side of the pool in a T-shirt and a pair of black cargo pants.

Her only response was to put her head down and keep pumping her arms and kicking her feet.

What is there to talk about?

Kai was about to become a dad to the Glamazon's baby. A child who would no doubt be a sugary slice of Anne Geddes newborn portrait perfection, given its genetic stock.

He'd been adamant that he wasn't in a position to get into a relationship. Now she understood why. He was on the precipice of entering into a lifelong connection with his child.

"Cam, baby, please get out. We need to talk."

Keep your head down and be like Dory. Just. Keep. Swimming.

Suddenly, she heard a huge splash. He'd stripped off his pants and shirt and jumped into the pool in his boxer briefs.

Kai wrapped his strong arms around her. He moved her to the edge of the pool, and stood her against the wall, his arms bracing the pool's edge on either side of her.

She slid the goggles on top of her head and wiped her face.

"*Really*, Kai?" she asked indignantly. "We've been working together, eating together, and making love all week, and now...*now* you want to have this conversation?"

He lowered his gaze for a moment before returning it to hers. "I fucked up, Cam. I realize that. I should've told you about my situation, but--"

"But you didn't. *Why?*" Her voice was louder than she intended. After all, his face was only a few inches from hers.

"I haven't told anyone besides my mother and brother. Mama Peaches doesn't even know." He dragged a hand down his face, wiping the water from his eyes. "I'm forty-fucking-years-old, Cam, and I'm out here fucking up like a frat boy. It's not something I'm proud of. Nor is it anything I'm sure of. I honestly wouldn't put anything past LaLa. You deserve better than this, Cam. I didn't want to drag you into my bullshit."

"I'm here, and I'm listening. So tell me now, Kai."

He sighed heavily, his gaze lowering. "Six months ago, it'd been a generally shitty week. We'd lost a big client here, I wasn't making a lot of headway in Chicago, my mom had a serious health scare, and to top it all off, it was the anniversary of my Dad's death." He rubbed his beard. "I wasn't taking it well. I was near the bottom of a bottle of Grey Goose when LaLa showed up at my door with a second

141

bottle. She said she knew it would be a hard night for me, and she wanted to make sure I was okay."

It obviously pained him to tell the story, but he forced himself to meet her gaze and continue. "She said I never really talked about my father. About what kind of man he was or what I remembered about him. So I started telling stories about my dad. Stories I hadn't thought about in years. We're laughing, and I'm choked up, and..."

"One thing led to another. Sounds familiar." Cam sighed. "Though you obviously weren't as careful with her as you were with me."

"Not true. I used a condom. I definitely wasn't that drunk. That's one of the reasons her story doesn't wash for me. I'm not saying it's impossible, but I need more than her word for it."

"You said that's *one* of the reasons you're having a hard time believing her story. There's something else, isn't there?"

Kai massaged his neck. "She'd been seeing someone else. The guy she left me for. He broke things off with her not long before we..." His voice trailed off and he sighed, shaking his head. "That's my brother's theory. My mother's theory is that this is about the money. LaLa squandered the lump sum settlement she got in the divorce, and she isn't entitled to alimony. I always wanted kids, but she wasn't ready for them." He shrugged. "My mother thinks this is LaLa's elaborate scheme to reclaim her cash cow."

"And what do you think?"

"To be honest, sweetheart, I'm not sure. It could be either or both. Or maybe this really is a series of unfortunate coincidences. But if the DNA test proves this is my son, I *will* take care of him, be there for him. And I won't ever allow him to feel like he was just some kind of mistake. Because, regardless of the circumstances, he deserves two loving, responsible parents. And I'll do everything in my power to fulfill my end of the bargain."

"You should've told me, Kai." Despite the cool temperature, her cheeks and face felt hot. Camilla's heart thumped in her chest, and a kaleidoscope of emotions cycled through her. Anger, hurt, disappointment, compassion, affection. And something that felt a lot like love.

"I should've. And I planned to tell you when you came down to the gym that morning. But then you insisted that this—" he gestured between them "--isn't anything serious. So I didn't see the point in telling you about my screw-up."

"I only said that because you were about to tell me again how you don't have room in your life for a relationship. A girl can only take so much rejection, Kai." She shoved a finger against his bare chest.

His eyes widened with realization. "So this *is* about more than just sex for you, too."

"Much more." Her voice was a whisper. "I honestly wasn't interested in getting involved with anyone. But then you walked into my life again and…" She shrugged. "I tried to hate you, I really did. But I just kept getting pulled deeper and deeper into your orbit and--"

"Everything changed." A slow smile spread across his handsome face as he cradled her cheek and dragged his thumb across her lower lip. "Same for me. I haven't been able to stop thinking about you since you handed me my ass in that town hall meeting."

"I wouldn't characterize it quite that way." *She totally would.* "But I haven't been able to stop thinking about you since then. Though I'm pretty sure it was the kiss that sealed the deal."

"That kiss." He grinned. "God, it killed me to go home to an empty bed after that amazing kiss."

"Me, too." Her gaze shifted to his lips involuntarily. She

looped her arms around his waist and pulled him closer, relishing the feel of him pressed against her.

"That's the whole truth, Cam. Every bit of it." He glided his fingers through her curls pulled into a one-sided pony-tail low at the back of her head. "So if you want to walk away right now, I completely understand. That won't affect my decision about our business deal. Because the truth is, after what I've seen this week, I'd be a fool not to work with you."

"You're kidding?" She suppressed a grin, excitement building in her chest.

"I'm not. And it's about more than just this past week. Before I left Chicago, I had the chance to visit several of the renovations your company completed. I watched your media interviews and appearances on the national do-it-yourselfer network. You're truly brilliant and immensely creative, Cam. I am so damn proud of you." A soft grin made him even more handsome. He leaned in and gave her a quick kiss, his lips salty with the water from the pool.

"I brought home two bottles of champagne, strawberries, and whipped cream to celebrate. One bottle to celebrate the deal I signed today. The other to mark the collaboration of Arrington Builders and Charming Home Design on the Marigold Circle project. The strawberries and whipped cream... Well, I'm sure you can use your imagination there."

A slow smile spread across her face and her skin heated. She was suddenly acutely conscious of his hardened length pressed against her belly.

"Thanks, Kai. You don't know how much this project means to me, to Uncle Lou, and to all of Southlake Park." She lifted onto her toes and he leaned down, his mouth meeting hers with another firm kiss as he pressed his large hands to her back.

"So that settles the question of our working together," he said tentatively, his eyes searching hers. "Now, about us...like

I said, no pressure. You're a busy woman on the threshold of amazing things. I know most people wouldn't choose to walk into such an unsure situation. A possible ready-made family. A sketchy ex. I'm the son of the man who wronged your family. And the asshole who blamed your father for wronging mine. There are so many reasons for you to walk away right now, Cam. I know that. So if you choose—"

"You." She pressed a hand to his cheek and smiled. "I choose you. And I have no intention of going anywhere. As long as you have room for me in your life, I want to be a part of it. And not just as friends. We'll face whatever comes together. But I have to know that you'll always trust me with the truth. All of it. I've worked too damn hard in my life to get where I am. I don't need any man to make my decisions for me. Not my dad, not Uncle Lou, and not you."

Kai sighed in relief. He nodded, his eyes searching hers. "Then in the spirit of full disclosure, there's one more thing I need to tell you."

Her heart beat faster and her spine stiffened. "Okay?"

"I love you." His eyes were filled with sincerity. "I'm pretty sure I started to fall for you the moment you stepped up to that podium."

Cam grinned, her eyes filled with tears. "And I love you."

Kai lifted her from the water and kissed her again.

She wrapped her legs around him and he leaned into her, her back pressed against the tiles of the pool. Her body tingled with her intense desire for this man who was no longer just her childhood crush or a business rival. He was the same boy she'd always loved. The one whose last name she'd appended to her own in scribblings at the back of her journal as a young girl.

"I'm about five seconds from ripping off this bikini," he whispered gruffly in her ear. "Let's take this upstairs. *Now.*"

"What about dinner?"

"We'll have it in bed. *Afterward*." His nostrils flared. "But right now, the only thing I want to devour is you."

A spark of electricity shot down her spine and made her keenly aware of the rising heat between them and the sensation of his body pressed to hers.

That was a collaboration she couldn't turn down.

MEKKAI

*M*ekkai sat in his truck outside the familiar house. It's paint job and brickwork as fresh as it'd been back then. As if it were completely unaffected by the time and turmoil that had passed since last he'd seen the place.

Time to man-up, Kai.

He sucked in a deep breath and stepped out of the truck. Kai plodded up the stone walkway toward the arch top wooden door with decorative black metal hinges and a speakeasy grill. He cleared his throat and rang the doorbell.

That was new. They'd switched the original doorbell for one of those new surveillance models.

There were muffled voices behind the heavy walnut door and then footsteps. Cammie swung the door open and smiled. As always, she was a breath of fresh air. A friendly-face before stepping before a much-deserved firing squad.

He swallowed hard, but forced a smile, leaning down to give her a quick kiss on her pink-glossed lips.

"You look beautiful," he whispered. "As always."

Camilla wore a casual, thigh-skimming, belted, denim

shirt-dress. She slipped her hands into the pockets of her dress, her head cocked. Her confident smile radiated strength and made him feel he could do anything, even this.

"Thank you, Kai. You look dashing this afternoon." She glided her fingertips beneath the slim lapels of his charcoal gray Hugo Boss suit. Her touch momentarily distracted him from the anxiety. She leaned in closer and whispered. "Take a breath. Everything will be fine."

She slipped her hand in his and they walked a few steps forward into the living room where Marianne and Michael Anthony stood. Marianne's hands were clasped tightly in front of her. Michael's were clenched in fists at either side.

Her father stared at their clasped hands, clearly disturbed that his daughter had broken rank and stood hand-in-hand with him, rather than shoulder-to-shoulder with her parents.

Cam's parents looked very much as he remembered. A little older, more gray hair and a few more fine lines, but otherwise very much the same.

"Mr. and Mrs. Anthony." He acknowledged both with a nod, his voice cracking slightly. As if he were a teenage boy showing up on their doorstep to take their daughter to the junior prom.

Not a good look, Kai.

"Mekkai," Marianne said tentatively.

Mr. Anthony simply nodded in response.

Kai cleared his throat and shoved his free hand into his pocket. "Thank you for allowing me the opportunity to come here and say this."

"And exactly what is it that you want to say, Mekkai?" Her father sank onto the sofa and her mother sat closely beside him, placing a firm hand on his knee. A silent plea for him to give Kai a chance.

She was throwing him a lifeline, and he gave her a quick nod in acknowledgement.

"Have a seat, Kai," Marianne said. It wasn't lost on him that she'd used his nickname.

"Thank you, Mrs. Anthony." It sounded oddly formal to address her that way when she'd once been Aunt Marianne.

He sat in one of the reupholstered wingback chairs. The chairs were too far apart for Cam to still hold his hand. She stood beside him instead, her hand still clutching his. But she remained silent.

This was something he needed to handle on his own.

"Mr. Anthony, first I want to tell you how deeply sorry I am for everything my father did. For the way he put your family's lives and livelihood at risk. For every false accusation he made against you. I would sacrifice *everything* to rewind the clock and erase all of the horrible things my father did to hurt your family and mine."

Her parents looked surprised. Marianne gripped Michael's hand, but didn't say anything.

"Thank you for the apology, son. But you don't owe me one on behalf of your father," Michael said. "Barris's mistakes are his own. You bear no responsibility for them. And I'd never hold anything he did against you."

Kai nodded, grateful for the man's words. "That's generous of you, Mr. Anthony. But still, on behalf of my mother, Keith, and myself, my family would like to extend our deepest apologies."

"Apology accepted," Marianne said.

"On a more personal note, I..." Kai stammered. The weight of his transgressions against this family, who'd never been guilty of anything but being true friends to his own, lay heavy on his chest. "I need to tell you how deeply sorry I am for every unkind word or thought I had about you. All these years, I honestly believed my dad was innocent. He swore to me that he was." He shook his head, his rising emotions choking his words. "It was foolish of me to blindly believe him. But regardless of what I personally believed, it doesn't excuse my poor treatment of you, your wife, and Cammie." He glanced up at her for the first time since he'd taken his seat.

She forced an encouraging smile even as silent tears stained her cheeks. Cam squeezed his hand, assuring him that she was fine and that he should continue.

When he glanced back at the Anthonys, Marianne was dabbing the corners of her eyes, too.

"I'm here to say I'm sorry for everything I did to hurt you. Especially for throwing that brick through your front window." He lowered his gaze. "I can't tell you how ashamed I am of my actions back then."

Kai reached into his breast pocket and stood, finally releasing Cammie's hand. He walked over to the man and extended a check to him. "This is for the damage I caused. I'm truly sorry to all of you—" he glanced back at Cammie "—for what I did that day. It was inexcusable."

"That isn't necessary, Kai," Mrs. Anthony said.

"Speak for yourself, woman." Mr. Anthony grabbed the check and Cammie laughed. His eyes widened. "Son, this is for $2,500. It's far too generous." He handed the check back to him. "You don't need to buy absolution, Kai. We forgive you, son."

Kai covered his mouth, his head bowed. A sense of relief washed over him. He extended his hand to the man.

Michael ignored his offered gesture. Instead, he stood and clutched Kai in a bear hug. He whispered in his ear. "We love you, son. We always have. Even through the worst of it."

Kai shut his eyes against the wave of emotion that filled his chest over this man's kindness and generosity. A man whom both he and his father had treated so unfairly. Yet, he'd given them nothing but love and support in return.

The older man finally released him. Kai hugged his wife, who waited patiently.

Marianne patted his back. "I know how hard that must've been for you. I'm proud of you, and I know your mother is, too."

He nodded, grateful for her kind words.

Kai turned to Cam, who jumped into his arms and hugged him tightly, her wet cheek pressed to his chest.

"I love you, Kai Arrington," she whispered, so that only he could hear her.

"Love you, too, babe." He kissed the top of her head.

Kai didn't know exactly what his future held. But whatever happened, he was grateful to have this incredible woman in his life again.

EPILOGUE

TWO YEARS LATER

*K*ai gripped Camilla's hand as Uncle Lou stood before the packed crowd at the Southlake Park Cultural Center. The very place where the two of them had first encountered each other after years apart. And the place where Cam had bid on Kai and won.

"We're standing up here today to celebrate all of the incredible renovations to Southlake Park that have happened over the past two years," Uncle Lou said proudly. "I'm so thankful to have been part of this renovation of our beloved neighborhood. Our home. The place that gave birth to and nurtured most of us here in this room. The neighborhood that made us who we are."

He paused, a broad smile on his face as the crowd whooped and cheered in response to his words. When the crowd settled down again, he resumed his speech.

"The slideshow you just saw chronicled all of the hard work and effort that your neighbors have put in to make Southlake Park what it is today. There are just so many people to thank for making this incredible transformation happen, but I'm just gonna start with the Mama of Chicago,

Mama Peaches Brighton, and her constant ace, Ms. Geraldine." He swept his hand toward the two women, seated on the front row just a few seats away from them.

Mama Peaches and Ms. Geraldine stood, nodding to acknowledge the crowd's standing ovation. Both women were dressed to the nines. Ms. Geraldine even had a brand-new wig. Though Cam was pretty sure she was wearing the thing sideways.

"I am grateful that my company, Lamberton Construction, has been given the honor of being the primary construction company working on the renovation of our little neighborhood." Lou paused again, nodding to acknowledge the crowd's applause and shouts of *thank you*. "But it has been one of my greatest honors to work with two phenomenal people, born of this neighborhood and living here once again, who have greatly contributed to the success of the renovation. Mekkai Arrington of Arrington Builders and his wife, Camilla Anthony-Arrington of Charming Home Design."

Applause went up in the crowd again. Kai stood, clutching Camilla's hand on one side while he cradled their five-month old son, Daniel Lamont Arrington, in the other arm. The child LaLa had been carrying was fathered by her ex. Something they hadn't learned until after the child's birth.

Something LaLa seemed to be aware of all along.

She'd been banking on Kai's desire for a family and any residual feelings he had for her. She hadn't expected Camilla to come along, or that she'd be determined not to let Kai's scheming ex come between them.

Kai and Cam returned to their seats, tears sliding down her cheeks. She was so grateful that after their stunning success with the Marigold Circle project, they'd been afforded the opportunity to collaborate on several additional projects in Southlake Park, Greater Chicago, and in Pleasure Cove where they lived part of the year.

She glanced back at her parents, Kai's mother, and both of their brothers and their families who'd taken time out of their busy lives to be here for the celebration.

Cam leaned in and kissed Daniel's forehead, then gave Kai a quick peck on the lips.

Life in Southlake Park was more than just good. It was everything she ever wanted and so much more.

ABOUT THE AUTHOR

Award-winning author Reese Ryan writes sexy, emotional, grown folks romance set in small Southern towns and filled with captivating family drama, surprising secrets, and complicated characters. She's the host of Story Behind the Story—her YouTube show where romance readers and authors connect.

A panelist at the 2017 Los Angeles Times Festival of Books, winner of an inaugural Vivian Award, and a two-time recipient of the Donna Hill Breakout Author Award, Reese is an advocate for the romance genre and diversity in fiction.

Visit Reese at ReeseRyan.com. Sign up for her VIP Readers email list for free reads and the latest news. Join her Reese Ryan VIP Reader Lounge for cover reveals, sneak peeks, reader give-aways, guest author takeaways, and more.

THE DISTINGUISHED GENTLEMEN SERIES

Have you read all of the books in the Distinguished Gentlemen series? This exciting, fourteen-author collaboration, brought to you by Book Euphoria, can be read in any order. Check out the additional titles in the series below.

Lover's Bid by AC Arthur
A Bid on Forever by Joy Avery
An Outlandish Bid by E.J. Brock
The Bid Catcher by Anita Davis
Switched At Bid by Nicole Falls
The Renegade Bid by Kelsey Green
The Contingency Bid by Sherelle Green
The Birthday Bid by Suzette D. Harrison
The Reluctant Bid by Sheryl Lister
Losing the Bid by Suzette Riddick
Invitation to Bid by Angela Seals
The Closing Bid by Elle Wright
The Alpha Bid by Ty Young

LET'S CONNECT!

Thank you so much for reading *The Rival Bid*! If you enjoyed Mekkai and Camilla's love story, please consider leaving a review on Amazon or Goodreads. Wondering what book of mine to read next? Try Quincy & Layla's story, ***Candidly Yours***.

Want to become a Reese Ryan insider?

Join my VIP Reader Lounge: http://bit.ly/VIPReaderLounge
Join my email newsletter list: http://bit.ly/VIPReaderList
Visit my website: ReeseRyan.com
Follow me on Instagram: https://www.instagram.com/
reeseryanwrites/
Subscribe to my YouTube show Story Behind the Story:
https://www.youtube.com/@ReeseRyanWrites
Follow me on TikTok: https://www.tiktok.com/@
reeseryanwrites
Follow me on Twitter: https://twitter.com/ReeseRyanWrites
Like me on Facebook: https://www.facebook.com/
ReeseRyanWrites/

ALSO BY REESE RYAN

EXCERPT: CANDIDLY YOURS

Layla St. John parked her late model, compact car in the expanded parking lot of Ms. Anna's Soul Food and Sweet & Savory Pies.

"It's cold as hell today," Nia, Layla's younger sister complained as she zipped her parka and pulled the hood over her head. "I hope Ms. Anna still has some chicken pot pies left. That would hit the spot right now."

"I'm trying to decide between that and the shepherd's pie," Layla said as they headed toward the restaurant.

A man stood at the counter laughing with Ms. Anna. He was tall with warm brown skin and short, thick hair cut into a fade. The leather jacket and distressed jeans fit his toned body just right. She could only see his face in profile, but there was something about his brilliant, genuine smile that was incredibly appealing.

Her sister's laughter pulled Layla out of her brief daze.

"Are you ogling that man's ass, Elle?" Nia used the nickname that Layla's family and friends called her. "I haven't seen you look at anybody like that in a minute. I was starting to think I needed to check your pulse." Her sister studied the man for a minute. "*Damn*. Bruh is fine. I see why he's got you all hot and bothered."

"Shh!" Layla held a gloved finger up to her lips. She'd been shushing her sister—nearly fifteen years her junior—for as long as Nia had been alive. "That glass isn't soundproof, you know."

"I'm sure he would appreciate the admiration." Nia winked, then swung the front door open before Layla had time to plead with her little sister not to pull any of her cutesy antics.

From what she could see, the man was handsome. And he had a heart-melting smile. Still, she wasn't into hook-ups.

Layla's fortieth birthday was just a couple of months away. If she was going to get involved with someone, it needed to be something real. Something with promise. The man talking to Ms. Anna was fine. And he had a body that reminded her that hers hadn't been...attended to by anyone with a pulse in quite some time. But he definitely gave off a hook-ups only kind of vibe.

Not what she was looking for.

Nia rushed inside, several steps ahead of her, just out of Layla's reach.

If she embarrasses me, I'm going to strangle her.

"Good evening, Ms. Anna." Nia waved innocently, drawing the attention of both the older woman who now owned the restaurant and the younger man she was chatting with.

"Nia, Layla. Good to see you both," Ms. Anna said. "And you both remember—"

"Quincy Johnston?" Layla froze where she stood as she studied the man's face.

He was much older now than when she'd last seen him as a shy teenage boy. He'd certainly matured. But those kind eyes and that signature smile were just as she remembered.

Why didn't I recognize him sooner?

"God, Layla." A slow smile spread across his handsome face as he ran a hand over his head. "I haven't seen you since—"

"You and Nolan's high school graduation." She grinned. "It's great to see you, Q."

Layla and Quincy exchanged a hug that felt awkward now that she realized that the full-grown, fine-ass man whose behind she'd been studying like it was the night before a finals exam was the childhood best friend of her little brother, Nolan. And a full ten years younger than her.

The fact that his strong arms and hard, toned body felt like her personal heaven and smelled like leather, sin, and something woodsy—a panty-obliterating combination if ever she'd smelled one—didn't help.

Layla's face was suddenly hot and her body tingled in places it definitely shouldn't. After all, Ms. Anna's was a family restaurant, not the strip joint at the edge of town. She extracted herself from his lingering hug, but not before she inhaled one final whiff of his cologne.

Maybe that made her a pathetic cougar, but she honestly couldn't help herself. At least she'd fought off the overwhelming urge to accidentally graze that round bottom with her fingertips.

"I see your body finally grew into that melon head." Nia folded her arms, one hip cocked. "Congratulations."

"Nia." Quincy chuckled, his voice so much deeper and sexier than it had been before—even after the awkward voice change of puberty. He gave her sister a quick hug.

Definitely nothing like the lingering, intimate hug he'd just given her. Not that it mattered or that she'd counted.

One Mississippi. Two Mississippi. Three Missi—

"Are you here for dinner?" Nia asked as soon as he'd released her.

"Yeah, I haven't had anything but coffee since breakfast this morning." He patted his belly. The sound drawing attention to his hard abs.

Layla sank her teeth into her lower lip and held back a quiet sigh. What the hell was going on with her tonight? She needed to get away from this man.

Right now.

"Well, Q, it was great to see you again," Layla was saying when her sister interrupted.

"It certainly is. You know, we were just about to sit down for a little Valentine's Day dinner, too. Why don't you join us?" Nia said. "Unless you already have plans. Are you meeting somebody? Your parents? Your siblings? A girlfriend? I assume there's no Mrs. Quincy since there's no ring on your finger."

"Nia," Layla hissed, elbowing her zero-filter little sister in the side gently. "Maybe Q would just like a little peace and solitude. Or maybe he has a Valentine's Day date he'd prefer not to tell your nosy behind about."

"I'd love to have dinner with you," Quincy's voice dipped lower when he responded to Nia's invitation. But his eyes were locked with hers.

Layla loosened the scarf around her neck and fanned herself with the collar of her shirt. Q, Nia, and Ms. Anna regarded her with knowing smiles. "It's hot in here with the ovens in the back, and I'm wearing a lot of layers right now." Layla's voice sounded way too defensive—even to her own ears.

Nia cackled and Ms. Anna could barely hide her grin. At least Q made the effort to hold back his smirk.

"Then let's grab a seat and get you out of all those clothes..." He cringed, and it reminded Layla of the shy little boy who'd often stumbled over his words. "I mean...your coat...obviously." Q cleared his throat. "Why don't you ladies grab a booth? I'll catch up with you. I just need to talk to Ms. Anna about something."

"Sounds good," Nia said, looping her arm through Layla's. "See you later, Ms. Anna!" she called over her shoulder.

"Nia Monique St. John what are you doing right now?" Layla whispered loudly as they headed for a booth.

"What you wouldn't," she replied matter-of-factly. "And you're welcome."

Read ***Candidly Yours*** today!

ABOUT CANDIDLY YOURS

He makes her an offer she can't refuse. She shows him everything he's been missing.

Layla St. John has the talent, creativity, and drive to start her own clothing line. What the big-hearted entrepreneur lacks is capital, because she's far too generous with her younger siblings. Still, when world-famous photographer Quincy Johnston—her youngest brother's oldest friend—wants to feature her in a photography series about carnival culture around the world, Layla's first response is no. She's happier behind the scenes. But when Quincy promises to help her get funding for her business, she reluctantly agrees to work on his project.

Quincy has spent the past ten years traveling the world, and he's made quite a name for himself. He's lived an isolated life free of deep connections. But a visit home to see his family and an encounter with the woman he's been crushing on since he was a pre-teen pierces the shell around his heart and gives him a taste of what he's been missing.

Can Layla and Quincy move past their relationship fears and take a chance on turning their short-term, secret fling into a shot at forever?

Get your copy of ***Candidly Yours*** now.

EXCERPT: SAVANNAH'S SECRETS

Despite the warm temperatures, the rain pelted her in cold sheets as she waded through the standing water. Her clothing was wet and heavy. Her feet slid as she ran in her soaking-wet shoes.

Savannah dropped into the driver's seat and caught her breath. Her eyes stung as she wiped water from her face with the back of her hand, which was just as wet.

She turned her key and gave the car some gas, grateful the engine turned over.

There was another flash of lightning, then a rumble of thunder, followed by a heavy knock on the window.

She screamed, her heart nearly beating out of her chest.

A large man in a hooded green rain slicker hovered outside her window.

She was cold, wet, alone and about to be murdered.

But not without a fight.

Savannah popped open her glove compartment and searched for something...anything...she could use as a weapon. She dug out the heavy tactical flashlight her grandfather had given her one Christmas. She beamed the bright light in the intruder's face.

"Blake?" Savannah pressed a hand to her chest, her heart still thudding against her breastbone. She partially lowered the window.

Even with his eyes hidden by the hood, she recognized the mouth and stubbled chin she'd spent too much time studying.

"You were expecting someone else?"

Smart-ass.

If she didn't work for the Abbotts, and she wasn't so damned glad not to be alone in the middle of a monsoon, she would have told Blake exactly what she thought of his smart-assery.

"What are you doing here? And where'd you come from?"

"I'm parked under the carport over there." He pointed in the opposite direction. "Came to check on the building. Didn't expect to see anyone here at this time of night in the storm."

"I didn't realize how late it was, or that the rain had gotten so bad. I'm headed home now."

"In this?" He sized up her small car.

She lifted a brow. "My flying saucer is in the shop."

"Savannah knew she shouldn't have said it, but the words slipped out of her mouth before she could reel them back in.

Blake wasn't angry. He smirked instead.

"Too bad. Because that's the only way you're gonna make it over the bridge."

"What are you talking about?"

"You're renting from Kayleigh Jemison in town, right?"

"How did you know—"

"It's Magnolia Lake. Everyone knows everyone in this

town," he said matter-of-factly. "And there are flash-flood warnings everywhere. No way will this small car make it through the low-lying areas between here and town."

"Flash floods?" Panic spread through her chest. "Isn't there another route I can take?"

"There's only one way back to town." He pointed toward the carport. "The ground is higher there. Park behind my truck, and I'll give you a ride home. I'll bring you back to get your car when the roads clear."

"Just leave my car here?" She stared at him dumbly.

"If I could fit it into the bed of my truck, I would." One side of his mouth curved in an impatient smile. "And if there was any other option, I'd tell you."

Savannah groaned as she returned her flashlight to the glove compartment. Then she pulled into the carport as Blake instructed.

"Got everything you need from your car?" Blake removed his hood and opened her car door.

"You act as if I won't see my car again anytime soon."

"Depends on how long it takes the river to go down."

"Seriously?" Savannah grabbed a few items from the middle console and shoved them in her bag before securing her vehicle. She followed Blake to the passenger side of his huge black truck.

She gasped, taken by surprise when Blake helped her up into the truck.

"I have a couple more things to check before we go. Sit tight. I'll be back before you can miss me."

Doubt it.

Blake shut her door and disappeared around the building.

Savannah waited for her heartbeat to slow down. She secured her seat belt and surveyed the interior of Blake's pickup truck. The satellite radio was set to an old-school hip-hop channel. The truck was tricked out with all the toys. High-end luxury meets Bo and Luke Duke with a refined hip-hop sensibility.

Perfectly Blake.

A clean citrus scent wafted from the air vents. The black leather seats she was dripping all over were inlaid with a tan design.

A fierce gust of wind blew the rain sideways and swayed the large truck. Her much smaller car rocked violently, as if it might blow over.

Another blinding flash of lightning was quickly followed by a rumble of thunder. Savannah gritted her teeth.

She'd give anything to be home in bed with the covers pulled over her head.

Everything will be fine. Don't freak out.

Savannah squeezed her eyes shut. Counted backward from ten, then forward again. When she opened them, Blake was spreading a yellow tarp over her small car.

Damn you, Blake Abbott.

She'd arrived in Magnolia Lake regarding every last one of the Abbotts as a villain. Blake's insistence on behaving like a knight in shining armor while looking like black Thor made it difficult to maintain that position.

He was being kind and considerate, doing what nearly any man would under the circumstances. Particularly one who regarded himself a Southern gentleman.

That didn't make him Gandhi.

And it sure as hell didn't prove the Abbotts weren't capable of cruelty. Especially when it came to their business.

But as he approached the truck, looking tall, handsome and delicious despite the rain, it was impossible not to like him.

Relax. It's just a ride home.

The storm had Savannah on edge. Nothing a little shoo-fly punch wouldn't soothe. She just needed to endure the next twenty minutes with Blake Abbott.

Download your copy of ***Savannah's Secrets*** today!